**THE DREAM IS ALWAYS THE SAME:**

We're trying to make our escape from Hell, millions of us streaming down the endless rows of gym lockers, past the searing lava showers, toward the glowing Open sign, and safety.

Behind us, the demons come. Some are clouds of acid fog; others are huge wolves or curiously mutated cats.

They're all chasing us, and they're all getting closer, and we're not all going to escape.

"We'll hold them here," Karl Cullinane shouts. "Who stands with me?"

The crowd rushes away, leaving some of us behind. . . .

# THE ROAD HOME

# THE ROAD HOME

*A*
*Guardians*
*of the*
*Flame*
*Novel*

# JOEL ROSENBERG

A ROC BOOK

ROC
Published by the Penguin Group
Penguin Books USA Inc., 375 Hudson Street,
New York, New York 10014, U.S.A.
Penguin Books Ltd, 27 Wrights Lane,
London W8 5TZ, England
Penguin Books Australia Ltd, Ringwood,
Victoria, Australia
Penguin Books Canada Ltd, 10 Alcorn Avenue,
Toronto, Ontario, Canada M4V 3B2
Penguin Books (N.Z.) Ltd, 182-190 Wairau Road,
Auckland 10, New Zealand

Penguin Books Ltd, Registered Offices:
Harmondsworth, Middlesex, England

Published by Roc, an imprint of Dutton Signet,
a division of Penguin Books USA Inc. Previously appeared
in a Roc hardcover edition.

First Mass Market Printing, July, 1995
10  9  8  7  6  5  4  3  2  1

This one's for three of my teachers:
Robert A. Heinlein, Donald Hamilton, and
David Drake.

# Acknowledgments

As usual, I'm indebted to the Usual Suspects—Bruce Bethke, Pat Wrede, Peg Kerr Ihinger—and even more than usually to my agent, Eleanor Wood; and I'm always grateful to my wife, Felicia Herman, and my daughters Judy and Rachel, for things that have both little and much to do with the work at hand.

# PROLOGUE

## The Road from Ehvenor

The truth is that the beginning of
anything and its end are alike touching.
—YOSHIDA KENKO

A hero's work is never done, which is
one of the minor reasons I don't
recommend the profession.
—WALTER SLOVOTSKY

Below, in the dark, in the city with the gleaming
building at its heart, the flickering had stopped.
But the killing hadn't.

He was supposed to feel a sense of satisfac-
tion, Jason Cullinane thought. But he didn't.
Whatever good he and the rest had done, they
had also loosed more violence upon the world.

Shit. Like there wasn't enough already.

And the cost . . . worst of all, it had cost them
Tennetty. But he would not cry over Tennetty.

Never. She was just his father's tame killer, that's all she had been, that's all she ever had been. She hadn't been his friend, not at all. It was just that she had latched onto him as the closest available substitute for Karl Cullinane.

*But I'm not Karl Cullinane,* he thought. *I'm just Jason Cullinane, I'm just eighteen years old, and I can't carry it all.* He realized that he had been unconsciously tightening, then loosening the shoulder muscles beneath his leather tunic. Mainly tightening. He felt like a lute string, wound too tight, ready to break at the slightest pluck.

He would not allow himself to break. That would not be permitted.

He almost jumped out of his skin when the dwarf patted him on the shoulder.

"It'll be okay," Ahira said. His face, broader than any human's could possibly be, was split in a grin that spoke more of relief than reassurance, although only his expression and the way sweat had slicked his hair down betrayed the exhaustion that the dwarf must have felt.

But he looked strange. Jason still hadn't gotten used to looking down at Ahira. Ahira had shrunk over the years in Jason's mind, if not in reality. Jason had known the dwarf for all of his life, and remembered looking up to him and wondering why all the grownups made short jokes about him, jokes that Ahira took not just with good grace, but with good humor, most of the time with a broad smile on his lips, all the time—at least in Jason's memory—with at least a trace of a grin.

In Jason's mind, the dwarf would still always tower over him, the way Ahira had when Jason was a baby, the way Ahira had loomed above him when Jason had taken his first steps toward those thick, hairy arms, toward the utter safety of those broad, strong hands. His father was gone too much of the time; Ahira had always been there. That smile had always been there.

"It'll all be okay. Trust me," the dwarf said, with just that trace of a smile.

Jason's mouth twisted. "I'll try."

Jason and Ahira had done their part, and the rent in reality had been sealed, and whether it was by Jason's mother or by the Three didn't really matter. It was done.

There was only a mess to be cleaned up, or lived with.

Below, the narrow streets of Ehvenor were filled with bands of the beasts Walter Slovotsky insisted on calling orcs, some fighting with each other, some fleeing into the countryside. Some sought the shelter of the hill, but it would be next to impossible to climb its rocky sides, and the plains and forest beyond the city were much more inviting than a narrow, twisting path up the side of a hill. They should be safe for now.

"Shit," Walter Slovotsky said. "Like closing the city dump and turning all the rats loose."

Not just orcs, either. Some immense creature, its broad side a glossy black in the starlight, slipped into the dark waters of the Cirric to disappear, only a momentary wake marking its passage. Another huge thing, misshapen and dark, flapped leathery wings as it vanished behind the city.

Jason turned his back on Ehvenor.

There were seven gathered around the hissing, spitting campfire. An elf, two dwarves, and four humans, if you included the Hand woman, who had no name and little of her own identity.

Mother, huddled in her blanket next to the campfire, was still weeping. Jason sat down next to her, put his arm around her, and pulled her close to him. What could he say? She had done it. She had brought Nareen's Eye close enough that the woman of the Hand could see and Vair the Uncertain could sear the rent shut.

It had been done, but Mother had spent not just her magic but her ability to do magic, burned it away to accomplish her goal.

Jason felt at the amulet around his neck. Nareen said that it would still work, that the sort of magic Mother had used to make it was mechanical, not transubstantive, but all Jason cared about was that it still worked, that it still protected him from being magically located as long as he wore it.

Jason looked over to where the Three stood. Nareen, the dwarf glassmaker wizard, rubbing a thumb idly against the side of his face: more aged and shriveled than any other dwarf Jason had ever met.

Vair the Uncertain, the elf: tall, rangy, and distant; under short, sharp bangs his eyes focused on something far away.

A nameless woman of the Healing Hand: watching the city with one eye of flesh and one Eye of glass.

Still Mother cried. Her shoulders shook with tears as she leaned close to Jason, seeking what comfort she could from his arm and shoulder.

Walter Slovotsky's all-is-wonderful-with-a-world-clever-enough-to-contain-Walter-Slovotsky smile was intact, and never mind that it seemed forced. They could all live with forced. His hands shaking only marginally, he reached into his pack and brought out a battered metal flask, then pulled the cork and drank deeply before passing the bottle to Ahira.

"Well," Ahira said, considering, "I think we earned that." He took a drink, then held the flask out toward the Hand woman.

She declined the offer with an upraised palm, her eyes, both real and glass, never leaving the pageant below. "Magical beasts loosed into the wild, into the earth and air and water," she said. She cocked her head to one side, and Jason wasn't sure, but perhaps there was a slim smile on her lips. Or perhaps not. "Things haven't been like this since I was a little girl."

She lifted a small bag to her shoulder, turned, and walked out into the night. It was all done so smoothly and casually that it was a long moment before Jason realized that she had left them.

Something bumped against Jason's arm. He looked up to see Ahira holding out the flask. Whiskey was not what Jason needed, and neither did the weeping woman leaning against his shoulder; he took the flask and passed it along to Nareen, who took a polite sip.

Vair produced a wire frame holding a clear red stone, and held it in the long fingers of his right hand, while with his left he threw a pinch of powder on the fire, then eyed the resulting smoke through his lens.

"It could be worse, perhaps," the elf said, his voice high-pitched but quiet, like the call of a distant hunting horn. "All of Faerie could have poured through, possibly. If the breach had not been sealed, if the one who cut the breach had not been stopped." He turned for a moment to Walter Slovotsky, and it looked like he was going to say something, but then the elf just tucked the ruby in his belt pouch, and left, vanishing in the darkness.

Really vanishing.

Jason turned to Ahira. Had anybody actually touched Vair? Had he really been here? He was going to ask, but there wasn't any point, and it didn't matter, not with his mother sobbing on his shoulder.

Why didn't somebody do something?

Nareen chuckled gently, for that is the way the Moderate People chuckle. "There is nothing to be done, young Cullinane. There is only much to be endured."

Nareen walked to the two of them and gently, slowly, pried Mother away from Jason, his fingers gentle against both Jason's arm and her shoulder, and took her small, delicate hands in his huge ones.

"You see," he said to Jason, although Jason couldn't figure out why Nareen would be talking to him, "those of us with the gift know a truth, that there is no pleasure quite like using it, like refining it." The dwarf's hands stroked hers in a way Jason tried to find offensive, perhaps almost obscene, but couldn't. "Most of us know that we must be careful in its use," Nareen went on relentlessly, "that if we use too much of the gift, push it too far, we will have to choose between it and sanity, and who would choose sanity compared to the glory of the power rippling up and down your spine, eh?"

Mother tried to pull her hands away from his,

but the dwarf held her tighter. Jason was going to say something, to interfere, but Ahira's broad hand was on his shoulder, and Ahira's face was grim.

"No," Nareen said. "You made your decision. To feed your power not with your sanity, but with your ability." A broad dwarven finger traced a red glow in front of her face. "Your ability to see this as sharp lines instead of a red blur, and all that implies. My compliments," he said. He eased her to the ground, and started to turn away.

But no—"Don't leave yet." Jason held up a hand. Mikyn was still running around loose, and he had to be found. "Wait. I—we, that is. We helped you. I'd like some help, from you." He swallowed. "There's a friend of mine, doing some horrible things. I need to find him. Help me." There were things he knew about Mikyn that nobody else did, that the abuse he had suffered as a boy was not just at his father's hands, but at the hands of an owner with perverted tastes. It had become, apparently, too much for him.

Ahira's gaze was frankly appraising. Was Jason insisting on this right now because of an obligation to Mikyn, or because he couldn't stand his mother's tears? He didn't have to voice the question; it might as well have been written across his forehead in big, blocky letters.

It was too bad that the answer wasn't.

*I'll tell you someday, Ahira, when I know. If I*

*ever know*. That was the trouble: if he couldn't tell when he was behaving nobly or selfishly, how could he expect others to get it right?

Nareen nodded. "Perhaps just a little."

"Okay."

Ahira was smiling at Walter Slovotsky, in that way that old friends smiled at each other in assurance and with reassurance. "What am I going to say?" he said.

Slovotsky returned the smile.

Jason felt more like an outsider than usual.

"Ask Jason," Slovotsky said. "It'll be good practice."

They were always trying to train him, and most of the time he didn't mind. This wasn't most of the time, but there was no point in arguing now. "That somebody has to take Mother home," he said, "but that I'm still too young and stupid—"

"Inexperienced," the dwarf said, interrupting.

"But close enough," Walter added.

It was what they meant anyway.

"—to be running around on my own." He swallowed, hard. "So," he went on, a catch in his voice, "one of you had better come with me. The one that's better at keeping out of trouble, not the one that's better at getting into it." Much better to be traveling with Ahira and not Slovotsky. There was going to be more than enough trouble between here and wherever Mikyn was.

"I wonder—who could that be?" Ahira's grin was almost infectious. Almost.

He turned to Slovotsky. "You'll watch out for Mother?"

"Sure," Slovotsky said. "Andrea needs some rest. The two of us, at least, had better camp here for tonight, head up into the hills tomorrow."

Jason tied his rucksack shut while Nareen made some arrangements with Walter Slovotsky.

Ahira nodded. " 'Twere best done quickly, eh?"

"There is that."

Slovotsky hugged him, and for the first time Jason realized how much he would miss the big man. There was something about him that was oddly reassuring. Maybe it was his easygoing self-confidence that would have bordered on egotism if only it could have been toned down. Or maybe not.

Slovotsky turned to Ahira, his grin still intact. "Watch your six, short one," he said. "And if you need me . . ."

Nareen and Ahira leading the way, they walked off into what was left of the night.

Behind them, Ehvenor stood in the dawn light, empty, no sign of life save for the gleaming building in its center.

# 1

## In Which I Have a Bad Dream and an Unpleasant Chat with an Old Friend

Sleep that knits up the ravelled sleave of
  care,
The death of each day's life, sore
  labour's bath,
Balm of hurt minds, great nature's second
  course,
Chief nourisher in life's feast.
—WILLIAM SHAKESPEARE

Will, your sister has an 800 number.
—WALTER SLOVOTSKY

The nightmare is always the same:

*We're trying to make our escape from Hell, millions of us streaming down the concrete corridors, past the open cells, toward the front gate, and safety. Bodies are packed tightly, too tightly, and it's all I can do to stay on my feet without knocking anybody else down.*

*Everybody I've ever loved is there, along with strange faces, some of which I know should be familiar. I can pick out the beefy face of Mrs.*

Thompson, my second-grade teacher, and I hold out a hand toward her, hoping to pull her close, but she's swept away from me into the crowd.

Behind us, there's a screaming pack of demons. Some of them are cartoons right out of Fantasia, and some are huge misshapen wolves like Boioardo. Others are just . . . different. There's one that looks like a human, except that he's got the head of a goat and an erect penis the size of my arm, and there's another that seems to be covered in boiling oatmeal, but they're all chasing us, and they're all getting closer.

One exit is up ahead: a steel door to the courtyard outside, dangling on its hinges.

The crowd pushes through.

I can't tell who's gone through, but I can only hope . . . Please. Let it be my daughters, my friends, the people I love. Please, God.

It occurs to me that I could be making sure that they're safe, I could be going with them, and who the hell told me my place was here?

There's a hand on my shoulder. "I did, asshole. Although I'm not the only one."

I'm not at all surprised to see Karl Cullinane standing there, surrounded by the rest of the legion of the dead. What surprises me is that his hair is gray as a winter storm cloud, and that his face is lined with wrinkles. He's at least sixty.

But . . . he can't be. He wasn't much older than forty when he died, buying the rest of us time to escape.

*Tennetty, her sneer as intact as her eyepatch, smiles at me out of a face that's withered and lined and just plain used up. "Who else would have, eh?"*

*Beyond her stands a company of old men, all dressed in white sailor's tunics. Some brandish swords, some spears, another a net and trident.*

*"Some work of noble note, eh?" The one who seems to be their leader takes a step forward. He's impossibly old; his face is deeply creased like ancient leather, and his hair and beard are white and fine as spun silk. But his back is straight and his high voice is clear as a glass of cold white wine. "Even fifty years ago, I could have held them by myself," he says. "But today, I will have your help, whoever you are."*

*Us help him?*

*I would tell him to go to hell, but, hey, what the fuck? We're already there.*

*Karl just clasps him on the shoulder. His voice cracks around the edges, not with fear, but with age. "We will hold the corridor," Karl says. "Who else is with me?"*

Then I wake up.

Back when I was a kid, sure as anything, the moment my temperature hit 103 degrees, the nightmares would come. Fever dreams, Stash and Emma used to call them.

Not the usual kind of nightmares, either—

familiar, reassuring things would turn dark and threatening, and somehow their familiarity was proof of the threat. The clock on the wall opposite my bed would stare down with a horrible, baleful glare, while I knew that just behind the open door to my closet misshapen things waited with evil intent, evidenced by the menacing way the shirts hung on their hangers, proven by the way a pair of pants lying on the floor huddled in a limp mass. I'd drift off to a light sleep without knowing it, and things would melt around me, while I'd huddle under the blankets, impossibly cold and wet with sweat, afraid to poke my head out.

A regular nightmare would go away by itself when I woke up, but not these fever dreams, not until the fever went below that critical temperature. And while just the touch of Mom's smooth, warm fingers to my forehead could dispel an ordinary nightmare, not even Stash's thick, callused hands could chase away the fever dreams.

It wasn't just that they were scary—everybody has nightmares, every now and then, but when you wake up, they're gone. What was horrible about it was that every time I'd close my eyes to sleep, the fever dreams would be there waiting for me, like some monster hiding in the dark behind a door.

I couldn't sleep; the bed was too comfortable, but the nightmares weren't. They were always the same, and I was always the same when I woke up, too sweaty to sleep, too scared to try, too tired to do anything useful.

At my movement, Aeia cuddled closer, her head pillowed on my shoulder, hair spilling like warm silk all over my neck and arm, her breath warm on my chest. The light of the candle sputtering in its pewter holder on the table next to our bed turned her face all lovely and golden. Not that it needed any help. High cheekbones, vaguely slanted eyes, rich, full lips making up the stubborn mouth that goes with being a Cullinane by birth or adoption . . . I would have pulled her closer, but I was bathed in enough sweat to mat down my chest hair, and I didn't think that cold and clammy was all that romantic.

What I really needed was to be held. I guess you never outgrow that.

Damn, damn, damn.

Back on the Other Side, I was an unusually big man, with all that implies. Not particularly clumsy, mind, but I was not overly graceful. I lost some size and bulk in the transition, and gained enough dexterity and deftness to be able to slip out of bed without waking her. Not that I had a choice, but even if I had one, I'd make the trade in half a second.

There's a lot I would have missed otherwise.

Too much.

I looked down at her for a moment.

Truth to think, if not to tell, I would have broken things off with Aeia and gone back to my wife. Or at least that was what I'd told myself. And even that was saying too much. I would have given up, or tried to give up, Aeia in my bed; I wouldn't have given her up as a friend. A lover, I can dispense with; somebody I love, no. I don't do that.

Shit, not even after they're dead.

*Tennetty, Karl, Chak, all of you . . . I miss you every minute.*

I slipped into a blousy pair of trousers, and noticed that I didn't have as much slack drawstring as I was used to. Hmm, my waist was starting to slip, just a little. Fifty more daily sit-ups perhaps, or maybe I could figure out some other exercise that would give me a flat stomach for another couple of years.

*Getting old, Walter,* I told myself, all too truthfully. It was hard to figure exactly, but I was more than forty years old, and definitely slowing down. Forty didn't seem so old, but shit, when I was a kid, I didn't think God was older than thirty. Maybe it wasn't quite yet time to give up this running around and getting in trouble, but the time was soon approaching. I'd been just a trace too slow in Fenevar, and that had endangered the others. If it wasn't for Ahira, if it wasn't for Tennetty, if it wasn't for Andy with a spell on the

tip of her tongue, we would all have died horribly
there.

Once more. One more time, maybe. Enough to
give Andy a chance to get out and get a taste of
it, then the worn-out ones of us could settle
down and turn things over to the younger crowd,
and those of their elders who still had it.

One more time, once to purge the nightmares,
and then I'd be done.

Jason was coming along, and hell, Thomen was
the Emperor. Over in Home, Petros was running
things mostly just fine, and Lou would still be active for the foreseeable future—the mid-forties
didn't make an engineer old—and who could tell
about Ahira? Dwarves didn't age much after they
reached maturity. A hundred and fifty, perhaps
two hundred years, then a quick decline to a dramatic senility, and then gone. How old was he?
Well, back on the Other Side, Ahira Bandylegs
had been thought of as not quite middle-aged.
For a dwarf, less than a hundred. Perhaps he had
another century in front of him, where I'd be
lucky to have another forty, fifty years.

Well, to hell with it. We all live under a death
sentence—and most of us under the Prisoner's
Dilemma. If worrying over it would do any good,
all humanity would be immortal, instead of most
of it being immoral.

Another English joke. The words for "immortal" and "immoral" in Erendra didn't sound simi-

lar. *Devorent* was a form of "to live," with the indefinite prefix; *enkeden* was a simple negation of *keden*. None of the locals would get it; they all tended to think in Erendra and not in English. Even Janie and the rest of the kids.

I don't know why that made me as sad as it did.

Never mind that. Once more, one more time to dispel the nightmares, and then I'd settle down. See if I could work some minor miracles with Imperial agriculture, or just ask Thomen for a ranch of my own. Surely the Empire owed me at least that much, I thought. Surely the Emperor owed me at least that much, I thought. Surely I owed myself that much, I thought.

Surely too much thinking was making me hungry, and thirsty. Even if U'len wasn't up yet, there would be something to eat in the pantry—maybe some slices off last night's joint of mutton, washed down with a glass of milk from the coldcellar.

Or a quick snort of Riccetti's Best. No. Best not to drink that if I was going to try to get more sleep. The nightmares were already bad enough.

I slipped a pair of throwing knives nevermind-exactlywhere, then opened the door no more than was necessary in order to slip out, preventing the hall lantern from shining down on Aeia's face. That might have woken her up, and she would have wanted to talk, and while I don't sleep with anybody I won't talk with, what I wanted now was some privacy and something cold to drink.

The hall carpet was soft beneath my bare feet.

Down the hall stood what had been my room, now officially occupied only by my wife, Kirah. Unofficially, that scumbag Bren Adahan was probably creeping down the hidden passageway from his connecting room to sleep with her, although perhaps that was just a passing phase. It wasn't being touched that made Kirah crazy, that triggered memories of things she wanted to forget.

It was being touched by me, but it wasn't my damn fault.

Or maybe it was; I guess it depends on how you look at it.

It would have been so easy to lose my temper, and I could have gotten away with that. Find your wife in bed with another man, be it in Holtun-Bieme or pretty damn near anywhere else, and few will blame you for killing them both in a white heat of anger.

It would be so easy.

But who was I kidding? There are problems that can be solved by kicking open a door and chopping everybody inside into tiny little bits, but no matter how I looked at it, no matter how shitty Kirah had made me feel, this wasn't one of those. We had been together for close to twenty years, had had two daughters, and in all that time, I'd never raised my hand to Kirah. Breaking a string like that by stabbing her and her lover in their bed wasn't really on the agenda.

Neither was slapping his face repeatedly, forehand and backhand, until I'd loosened every single tooth and he looked like he had a mouthful of bloody Chiclets.

Although it did make me feel good to think about it.

*Sublimate, sublimate, dance to the music . . .*

I headed downstairs, and at the bottom of the stairs, started toward the kitchen and pantry, only to freeze at the sound of a voice behind me:

"Late night, again?" Doria Perlstein, her legs curled up underneath her, was sitting on an oversized, overstuffed chair at the end of the downstairs hallway, which sounds like a stranger place to hang out than it is. That end of the hallway had long—back a couple of Furnaels or twelve—been a sitting area, where the lady of the house could sit and knit or chat and take tea, all the while keeping an eye on the staff bustling in and out of the kitchen, without them being right in her lap. Doria had a stack of papers on an ancient lapdesk. All governments, even that of Barony Cullinane, live on paper, I guess, and I didn't have reason to doubt that the regent would have it any different.

"Well," I said, shrugging, "yeah."

"Not surprised. Seems to run in the family."

"Oh?"

"Your youngest wandered down a while ago. I sent her to the kitchen."

"My baby daughter's sleeping in the kitchen," I said, trying for a deadpan delivery to let the words speak for themselves.

Doria smiled. "U'len's watching over her. She rigged a nice little spot between the oven and the woodbin, protected by a bit of latticework—when the oven's low, it keeps things toasty warm. I wouldn't worry."

_It's not your daughter,_ I didn't say, and not because Doria couldn't have children. She would no more have let Doranne sleep in unsafe proximity to a stove than I would, so I just let it drop.

Doria was dressed in a thin black robe, belted tightly around her waist, that made her normally pale skin seem wan, except that the smoothness of her complexion and the hints of highlights at the cheekbones turned it all smooth and creamy. She adjusted the cleavage at the opening of her robe for a moment, then smiled up at me.

"Not fair to tease the animals, Doria," I said, although that was just for effect. Doria and I had long since worked out that being friends worked better for us than being lovers, and what with things being new for Aeia and me, I wasn't exactly suffering.

"Pity." She tossed her head, once, flirtingly, clearing the fringe of blond hair from her eyes. Most women look better to me with long hair, but there was something about the way her short hair flipped from side to side that was particularly pretty, and kind of young, a strange contrast to her wide eyes with their golden irises, eyes that seemed to be ancient.

"You know the difference between your friends and your partners?" she asked, a slight smile on her full lips.

"Which kind of partner?"

"Ahira, Karl, Chak, Tennetty—that kind."

"Yeah: some of my friends are lovely; those kinds of partners aren't."

She shook her head. "It's the eyes. You and Ahira almost never look each other in the eye. I used to think it was that you were afraid to, but I was wrong. You're each always standing watch, and you know in your heart and your gut that you don't have to watch each other, so you unconsciously divide the universe into the part that you watch over and the part that your partner watches over, like the rest of the universe is the enemy."

"Sometimes . . ." I started to say something, but I didn't quite know what. "Sometimes the rest of the universe is the enemy, kiddo." Slovotsky's Law Number Sixteen: When the universe doesn't give a fuck, don't be mad: it's being as friendly as it ever gets.

"Sometimes it's just the job that is the enemy." She tapped a fingernail on the paper spread out on her lapdesk. "Running a barony is a fair amount of work."

"Think Jason might keep you on after he gets back?" I asked.

"Could be." She shrugged. "I've had better jobs, although not recently," she said. A smirk quirked across her lips for just a second until it could become a smile. She carefully stacked the papers, then set the lapdesk down on the table at her elbow. "Not that I've gotten a lot done tonight. I haven't been able to concentrate tonight, anyway. I was wondering when you'd show up," she said.

"I'm that predictable, eh?"

Everybody I love has at least one habit that drives me absolutely bugfuck, even though I try not to show it. With Ahira, it's his stubborn unwillingness to admit the obvious and insist that I do. With Janie, it's that she's always a step ahead of me. With Doria, it's her habit of changing the subject from light to serious.

"No," she said, sobering irritatingly. "But I've been talking to Aeia. More to the point, she came to me. Says you've been having trouble sleeping."

I shrugged. "Happens, off the road." Each of us grows our own night demons; mine bother me when I'm in a soft bed at home, even if the home wasn't technically mine, but the property of the Cullinane barons. My subconscious only deals in technicalities when it's holding them against me.

She shook her head. "That isn't going to fly." She licked her lips, once, and then pursed them for a moment. "You're eating like a horse, and I'm given to understand you're getting regular exercise," she said, quirking a smile, "both in and out of bed."

"And with enough food, exercise, and sex, all is well for the forty-year-old male, is that it?"

"Well, no. Not if he's having a midlife crisis."

I had to laugh. "Excuse me?"

"Oh, come on. Put it in Other Side terms. Take, say, an agricultural consultant to a major monarch." She stopped herself, and chuckled. "Okay, make that an agricultural consultant to, say, a state governor. He's got a wife and two kids, a stable job that pays well, and an equally stable—if perhaps a trifle dull—lifestyle. Less than a year later, he finds himself out in the world in a whole new job that involves getting shot at, and he's dumped his wife for a younger woman, and even figured out a way to blame her for it. What would you call it?"

"Not fair. You're ignoring the specifics."

She waved it away. "There're always specifics. You think most middle-aged men in the midst of a midlife crisis—"

"You missed a 'mid' in there, maybe."

"—think they're picking up a random young bimbo as a new bed partner?"

That got me angry. "I don't want you talking about Aeia like that."

She sniffed. "I'm not talking about her, you idiot; I'm talking about *you*. You can't see it as part of a pattern. It just *has* to be something special between you and her, something precious.

"What's precious, just maybe, is that she's somebody new, somebody younger, somebody who makes you feel younger, because what it's all really about is that you feel the breath of your own mortality on your neck, and you've got to run faster, to strike out in some new direction to try to escape it."

I don't really know whether her smile was intended to be mocking, but it was infuriating. "And if the model doesn't fit perfectly, what model ever has?"

I guess Doria has more than one habit that irritates me.

# 2

## The Apprentice Warrior

It is easy to fly into a passion—anybody can do that—but to be angry with the right person and at the right time and with the right object and in the right way—that is not easy, and it is not everyone who can do it.

—ARISTOTLE

When it comes to throwing a fit, it's better to give than to receive—and much the best to avoid the whole thing entirely.

—WALTER SLOVOTSKY

The air in the thatch hut was cool and quiet; the killing had been over a long time. But it didn't feel that way. It hadn't felt that way before, and it didn't now.

"Ta havath, Jason," the dwarf said. Literally, it was the verb *to maintain* in Erendra, but it meant *take it easy. Relax. Don't get excited.* "It happened a long time ago." His voice was quiet, but rasping, the sound of an old saw, still sharp.

"Too long," Jason Cullinane said, bending to

feel at the rotting straw covering the floor. Soggy, more than half-rotted, it had not been changed in many tendays.

The shack was dark, and quiet, and no longer reeked of death, as though it never had. If anything, it smelled too good. The damp, musty reek of the thatch overhead, the fresh wind blowing in the open door and out through the torn greased paper that had covered the window, and the cool smells of the forest all combined with the rotting straw in a way that was disturbingly pleasant.

It should have smelled of death.

An old man and an old woman had been killed here, murdered here.

*By my best friend,* he thought. *Mikyn . . .*

Enough. Straightening, he turned to the dwarf. Ahira's easy good humor hadn't deserted him, not even here and now as he stood where morning sunlight splashed golden on the rotting straw. There was nothing of a broad smile on his face, but just a trace peeked through his black beard. It held something of reassurance in it, perhaps, and perhaps more than something of an announcement, perhaps something of a warning.

It said, *I have dealt with worse than this, and this too I will deal with.*

Jason envied his self-assurance.

"There's nothing more we can do here," Ahira said.

"More?"

Ahira's laugh might have been forced, or perhaps not. It was hard to tell. "Nothing, then."

They exited into the too-bright sunlight. Nareen was waiting out there, floating comfortably in the air above the three battered rucksacks. The wind kept the grasses waving gently, like the Cirric on a quiet day, but it didn't appear to affect Nareen. Little did.

His appearance was exceptional for a dwarf. While he had the large bones and even larger joints of his breed, Nareen lacked the huge bundles of muscle that generally wrapped around a dwarf's bones. His skin hung on him loosely, as though he was somehow deflated. Instead of the gentle rounding that softened the harsh bones of Ahira's face into something warm and familiar, Nareen's cheekbones and eye ridges kept his look almost skeletal. It was like having a skull looking out at you, and Jason didn't like it much at all.

"There is, I take it, no sign of your friend?"

Jason shook his head. "None." He had hoped to find some trace of Mikyn, something he had left behind, something that Nareen could use to trace him, but it had been unlikely, and it was too much to ask. But maybe, just maybe.

He had the beginning of an idea, but it was one that scared him silly. It probably required more cleverness, or more fighting skills, than he would ever have. But it made sense, at least on one level, and it was the sort of thing that Walter Slovotsky would think of.

Purely logical: who else was looking for Mikyn? The Slavers Guild was, and they were based in Pandathaway. That might be the place to find out where Mikyn was—although it was also a place where Jason and Ahira were wanted, dead or alive. It would take much trickiness to get in and out alive. More of a Walter Slovotsky thing than a Jason Cullinane thing.

Leave it be, for the time being.

# 3

## In Which I Hurt Myself for Good Reason, and Play with Knives

Perhaps the reward of the spirit who tries
is not the goal but the exercise.
—E. V. COOKE

Well, truth to tell, my first thought
after we arrived on This Side wasn't *Holy
shit—I'll never have to do a fucking
calisthenic again.* It was, however, my
second thought. (I was wrong, but
there you have it.)
—WALTER SLOVOTSKY

I never really wanted to be a football player, but
my scholarship was a way for me to go to college
without sucking Stash and Emma's savings dry.
They'd put aside money for it, sure, but Other
Side colleges are like the vampires that leaked
out of Faerie during the Leak: how much of your
money they soak up isn't a variable—they take *all*
of it. That's the way the system is structured.

There are a few situations where some of that
weight will be taken off you. It happened to some

of us. Lou Riccetti got a thousand bucks a year off of his tuition for being a National Merit Finalist (never mind what that means; it's a long story). I never asked James Michael what sort of deal he got, although I know there was one.

Me, I got a completely free ride for being very adept at running after and seizing a fast-running man holding an inflated pig-leather bladder, and then quickly throwing him to the ground. In order to maintain that facility, I had to spend a lot of time with sweaty people of varying intelligence, all of whom were obsessed with the movement of that leather bladder, and with training for their opportunity either to move it or to prevent somebody else from moving it.

I dunno, but it seemed reasonable to me. At the time.

By the time I had reached a hundred sit-ups, my abdominal muscles were screaming for mercy, so I decided to inflict only another fifty on them.

The trick is to persuade yourself that every bit of pain is helping make things better, and for all I know that can be true about a lot of things.

That which does not kill me makes me stronger, and all.

Or maybe it just hurts. I don't know.

Dressed in a pair of drawstring shorts and a loose shirt, I was stretched out on a woven grass mat in the fencing studio near the window at the juncture of floor and ceiling. The early morning sunlight had warmed the mat to merely chilled, which I could live with, and it made the wicker walls look all cozy and golden, which I could enjoy.

"Whatcha doing, Daddy?" came from the entrance to the fencing studio, in a high-pitched voice that still didn't have a full grasp of complex consonants. My baby daughter, Doria Andrea.

Well, at least that was better than the time that Janie had walked in on Kirah and me making love, and said the same thing, followed somewhat later by, "If you were having so much fun, why aren't you smiling?"

My daughters seem to catch me off guard when I'm sweaty; I was grateful this time it was only from exercise.

She was in a sort of shorts-based overall today, over a dingy white pullover sweater with the arms rolled up. I bet that even the dingy whiteness wouldn't last until lunch; my daughters always play hard, and there was a new coal-black foal in the stable that Doranne was helping the stable boy take care of, help that probably only slowed him down a medium amount. Which, too, was okay.

"Hi, Doranne," I said, sitting up to give her a hug. Attention fathers: enjoy the hugs while you can; eventually they get too old for that, or at least think they're too old. "I'm staving off eternity, one bit of agony at a time."

She frowned, but then put the frown away. When you're four, adults are always saying things that you don't understand, but if you let them know that, then they'll always say, "You'll understand when you're older."

Except me. I *never* say that to my kids.

"I don't understand," she finally said.

"What I meant to say is that I'm exercising, trying to keep myself strong and pretty. What's up?"

She didn't get that, but she decided that it didn't bother her. Which also was okay.

"Uncle Bren said to tell you he wanted to see you," she said.

Which wasn't okay. And which also wasn't her fault. "Thanks, honey," I said. "Did he say where he'd be?"

She shook her head. "I din't ask. I'm sorry."

"T'sokay, kidlet," I said. "You seen Auntie Andy this morning?"

She nodded. "I helped her saddle her horse; she went for a ride."

Well, that was good. By far, the best intermediate training in riding consists of riding a lot, and I had prescribed long, hard morning rides for Andy, switching horses out at the farm, and then again at one of the nearer villages. It would be good for her seat—technical term—and I couldn't help thinking what it was doing for her thighs, then mentally slapped myself. Life was complicated enough.

My daughter shifted from foot to foot.

"What is it?"

"Dier said that if I went to the stables early enough, I could feed the new baby horse."

"Then you'd better get going," I said, giving her a quick squeeze before I let her go. "I'll go find the baron."

She left at a dead run. Kids always run, and think nothing of it.

In the corner of the room, right over the sump-drain, was a cold-shower stall. I tossed off my exercise clothes, unstrapped the scabbard from my right calf, then quickly sluiced myself off in the cold water, fed from the cistern on the roof. Rain-water's good for the hair, so I'm told, but it was cold enough to make my testicles try and crawl back up inside my body cavity.

I dried myself with a thick but napless towel.

Time to get dressed. I was breaking in a new pair of black leather trousers, so I slipped those on, and tucked in the tails of an all-too-white silk shirt before belting it tightly around my waist.

The back of the matching leather vest held one throwing knife; the other one returned to its usual spot strapped to my calf. I slipped a Therranji garrote into a hidden pocket at the inside of my vest, then belted on my weapons belt, sword on the left, its hilt properly canted forward, a single pistol on the right.

Not quite what I'd prefer to take with me to have a talk with my wife's lover, but then again, I wasn't particularly expecting violence. Frankly, I was willing to bet against it. I didn't know whether or not I could have taken Bren in a fair fight, but it would have been a stupid gamble for either of us. Having his blood on my hands was unlikely to make me popular with my soon-to-be-ex-wife, or with any of the other women around —forgetting what the Emperor would probably say about me killing his favorite Holtish baron. And there are people who wouldn't have taken kindly to him killing me, probably including Kirah.

There are, after all, an amazing number of problems in the world that can't be fixed by slitting the right throat.

I loosened my sword in its sheath and headed out into the day.

The three musketeers caught up with me in the courtyard of the main keep, just outside of the back entrance to the kitchens, right where the cooks were growing yet another patch of dragonbane. (Well, with all the strange things that had been leaching out of Faerie, I didn't have a lot of trouble seeing why the cultivation of the stuff was becoming popular again. It's poisonous to most of the magical metabolisms.)

Well, not really the three musketeers. Which is just as well. Shit, imagine actually having Athos, Porthos, and Aramis at your back in a fight. By the time they'd finished speechifying, and then elegantly drawing their swords, and then preparing to fence—each in a style designed to reveal the nature of his character—three tired, ordinary swordsmen would have been looking down at their dead, bleeding bodies, breathing through their mouths to avoid the stink in the air, and wondering why life couldn't always be this easy.

Me, I'll take Kethol, Pirojil, and Durine.

Kethol: raw-boned, red-headed, and lanky, with deep-set eyes that alternated between staring off in whatever direction he had last been looking and constantly moving, constantly searching, although for what, I'd never been able to ask.

He noticed me noticing, and let or forced an easy grin across his face.

Pirojil: broad and squat, with a huge flattened nose, massive jaw and overhanging eyeridge. The top half of his right ear was gone; it looked like it had been chewed off, which could easily have been the case. His neck was too thick, and his receding chin was only one of several chins. Pirojil was probably the ugliest man I'd ever met, but with a broad smile that made his face comfortably homely, as long as you didn't look right at it.

I didn't. But he was watching me.

And then there was Durine: the big man, almost a head taller than Kethol. Bushy beard and unsmiling mouth on a face sitting over a bull neck; a chest like a beer barrel, thick, hairy arms, and huge, blunt fingers that seemed too wide to be adept with anything subtler than a club. Not particularly well-proportioned—his legs were just an irritating amount too short for his body—not particularly clever, not particularly friendly, and not particularly even-tempered.

And looking at me in a way that was not particularly pleasant.

More than two dozen men had set out with Karl on his Last Ride. These three had survived. Part of it was luck, I'm sure, but not all of it. There was something about them, something that smelled of death, maybe, and of suffering, and of men who had seen and done things that bothered them, but that they had lived through, and they could live through whatever they had to do to you, thank you very much.

Which is why I might have chosen them as bodyguards, but I didn't particularly like them.

Kethol leaned against a whitewashed wall, still chewing on a few slivers of flesh clinging to a drumstick from either a large capon or a medium-sized turkey.

He gestured with it. "A moment of your time, Walter Slovotsky?"

I liked that. Neither my name nor my effective position really fit into their view of the world, so all three of them called me by my full name, pronouncing my first name as though it was a title.

I dialed for an easy smile. "Of course, Kethol. What's going on?"

Durine spoke up, his voice a bass rumble, threatening a thunder that only sounded distant. "The Regent asked us to have a word with you. And perhaps one with the Baron Adahan, as well." His hands gestured clumsily, as they usually did when they weren't holding something that could stab, cut, or crush. "She says she wouldn't want any accidents to happen."

I held up both hands. "Ta havath, eh? I don't want a fight, any more than he does." Which was true, although I probably should have kept the anger out of my voice, if I wanted to be believed. Which I did.

Kethol nodded, trying to look as though he believed me. Durine's face held no expression.

Pirojil just looked skeptical. And ugly. "Things have been known to get out of hand."

"As we should know," Durine said, rubbing one huge finger against an old scar—not one I'd given him. I'd sparred with each of the three of them, but never with anything more than practice weapons, and never with any intention more serious than a good workout. Look, if I have to fight, my preference in an opponent would be a lame, one-legged, arthritic swordsman with cataracts and palsy—I don't need a fair fight, thank you very much.

Pirojil chuckled, and in a moment, Kethol joined him. Not one of the three offered to explain it to me. I hate in-jokes.

"Then you wouldn't mind the three of us keeping company with you for a short while on this fine day?" Kethol asked.

Sure. Just what I needed. Three large, murderous babysitters.

It didn't seem politic to refuse. And, besides, I was going to be doing a spot of adult babysitting myself. "Sure," I said. "You don't mind hitting the kennels first."

May as well let them in for the hard time as well as the good, although given what they'd been through from time to time, a bit of wolf dung wasn't going to be all that difficult to deal with.

I was surprised to find my daughter Janie in the kennels, but I shouldn't have been. She had been spending a lot of time with Nick and Nora, and they would always whine and whimper when she left them in their kennels.

Well, kennel is the best term, I guess, although it wasn't where the castle dogkeeper kept the dogs. The castle dogs didn't take to being kept near wolves, and if kenneled near Nick and Nora, would alternate between cowering in one corner of their cells and barking up a storm.

Which wasn't the only reason that the two of them had been moved to a newly built structure in an unused corner of the keep. There had at one point been something there; a rough inlaid-stone floor sprawled out beyond the edges of the wolf pens. Just as well. Wolves dig, and dig well.

What Doria had ordered built filled the bill nicely, even if a six-foot-high wire fence looked out of place in the castle. The wolves didn't like the feel of the wire against their paws, and it hurt to try to climb it.

Janie had been feeding them over by their Snoopy-style doghouse, but they raised their heads at our approach and bounded over to the gate, waiting, tails wagging, Nick's thumping against the fence post with a rhythmic _clinkity-clinkity-clinkity_ until Janie opened the fence and let them come out and greet me.

The three musketeers didn't like all this. Hands tended to hover near hilts, and the wolves didn't like the movement. Janie—like me—was part of the pack, but not the three of them.

She caught the movement and gave Nora a loud thump on the back. "Down, down, they're okay. You just leave them alone," she said, the voice of authority.

Teenage daughters are a problem. Today she was dressed in an imitation of Andy's leather road outfit: jacket-vest tight, midriff bare to equally tight leather jeans. With the rough boots and the addition of the leather overjacket now hanging on a fence post, it wasn't a bad outfit for running through the fields and woods with a pair of wolves, but it reminded me more than I was comfortable with that she had long since ceased being a girl and was well into woman.

While the outfit wasn't an invitation to rape—there's no such thing as an invitation to rape—it was an invitation to being hit on, even when her ensemble also included a pair of very territorial wolves. Just as well I don't really care if my daughter fools around.

She gave me a quick hug and a kiss—okay, she was still my baby, after sixteen or so years, although baby fat had long since given way to long, thin limbs, and chubby cheeks to a heart-shaped face framed in straight, short, black hair.

"Hi, Daddy."

"Hi, Sweetie. And Nick, you're not my type. Go away."

Dogs, wolf or tame, are never an aid to personal dignity: Nick, always the more affectionate of the two, stuck his nose in my crotch as a demand to be petted. Or thumped, more precisely. It was like patting a fur-covered wall. His fur was as thick as steel wool, and almost as stiff. Fingers couldn't penetrate through to the flesh, and it would give even teeth a hard time. Which was the whole point of it, I suppose.

Nora took her time coming over to give me a sniff and a lick, but seemed to take a few quick pats with pleasure. It's important to remind the furry little buggers every now and then that you're the boss, because they tend to forget.

Which, as usual, is something they were working out. Nick gave a quick snarl at her, his tail erect, teeth bared. Seemed he didn't want to share me with her.

Janie glared at me, then reached over and smacked him firmly on the head. *"No."* She jerked her head at me. "You tell him, too, Daddy."

I did, then cocked my head at her.

She sighed. How could a father be so ignorant of the obvious?

"It's okay for them to work out who the boss is in private, but not in front of you. If Nora needs to be put in place while we're around, *we* do it, not Nick." She gave him a dramatic glare. "Down, Nickie, *down*," and the huge creature immediately crouched, looking for all the world scared of the teenaged girl who surely didn't weigh more than half of what he did, and didn't come equipped with a tenth of the natural weaponry.

Well, I was impressed, and the three soldiers at least had the grace to appear to be. "Nicely done, child of mine."

Her dimples were still as cute as they'd been

when she used to wet on my lap. "Thanks, Daddy. Something you needed to see me about?"

"I figured I'd stop by on my way to find Bren Adahan," I said.

She looked disappointed—"And you want to set the dogs on him? Not fair, Daddy, not fair at all."—but then realized that she was overdoing it, and broke into laughter.

"It's not funny."

Janie shook her head. "It had best be funny, Daddy. Otherwise it's going to be too sad. You and Mother have been together how long? And now things are going to fall apart just because you can't keep it in your pants?"

Pirojil snickered at that, which gave me somebody else to glare at.

"It's a lot more complicated than that, kiddo."

"It always is, I hear—and touchy, aren't we?" She shrugged, but then smiled to take the sting out of it. "But so what?—Bren should be down by the stables; he was talking about riding out to the farm. Said that it's the baron's job to look in on things from time to time, and that if Jason's not going to do it, he'll do it for him."

Kethol was already in a jog toward the stables, calling out for four horses. I shrugged and gave my daughter a peck on the head, before following.

"Play nice, Daddy."

Janie always gets the last word.

\* \* \*

We caught up to Bren Adahan at the apple orchard outside the farm—the family farm was an old baronial tradition, going back at least several generations of Furnaels.

Most ruling nobility lives totally as either symbiotes or parasites—take your pick, depending on whether or not you think the ruling class does something for its keep. (I do—I just think they do it all too often.) Taxes consist of taking a portion either of the peasant farmers' money or—more often—of what they grow, and, typically, that's the only thing that the ruler lives off.

The Furnaels had always done things differently, just a bit. Much of the farmland right around the keep was owned and kept in operation by the family itself—or, to be more accurate, by family retainers, farmers who, historically, worked the baron's lands as what I can best describe as collective crofters.

Not the best deal in the world for them, mind, but it did mean there was always a default local occupation for the odd somebody—a farm can't always use a lot more help, but it can always take on another one or two—and it left the crofters less likely to be wiped out during hard times, as the baron had a direct responsibility for their welfare. They "ate from his table" in legal theory, if rarely in practice.

The best part of the deal for the crofters, of course, was during wartime, when crofters had both the right and—more important!—the chance to seek sanctuary in the keep.

During times of peace, that didn't seem like so much, but memories of the Holtun-Bieme war were still fresh in some minds, and in some of the scars that still showed—in the newish split rail fences that stood where old stone fences should have; in wattle-and-daub houses whose beams looked too new, too unweathered; in the short green scrub that stood where tall, wind-breaking patches of trees should have, and in young apple orchards where the trees were only now beginning to bear fruit.

The Holtish had rampaged through the territory, burning what they couldn't pack away. If Karl hadn't stopped them, the Biemish would have returned the favor just a few miles away, across the river in Barony Adahan . . .

Part of the tradition was for the baronial family to take a hands-on attitude with the farming, and while Bren Adahan was not, strictly speaking, a member of the family, he was helping to fill in. He took the job seriously enough to be stripped to the waist and halfway up one of the few remaining ancient apple trees, cutting grafts from the newer shoots high up.

An apple tree, at least a Biemish apple tree, was as much a work of art as of nature. Some of the least interesting apples bred true—the sour little things called, as close as I can translate it, old-maid's apples, the crisp but almost tasteless horse-apple, the pig's apple—but the better ones were hybrid, and the better hybrids came from trees with several different styles of cuttings.

Hence the grafting.

I didn't know the names of the fifty or so workers in the fields—hey, they weren't *my* peasants—but I did hear whispers involving my name, as though it was some big deal that Walter Slovotsky would be here.

Fame is a bit weird.

As the three musketeers and I approached, Bren, sweat-slick from headband to the dark stains spreading down the sides of his legs, dropped a bundle of freshly cut shoots to waiting hands below, then dropped lithely from the tree and rose easily to his feet, taking a long swig from a proffered waterbag.

"I told Doranne that I'd make an effort to see you later," he said, still sweating, but not panting. The sun was hot and the morning was going to give way to noon, but the bastard wasn't really tired, just sweaty.

I think I resented that more than I should have.

He poured some water into one hand and splashed it on his face to clear the sweat away from his eyes.

"You sent for me," I said. "I'm here."

He eyed his weapon belt, dangling from a tree

a good leap away, and then looked back at me. "I would have thought you'd think yourself enough to take anything on, Walter Slovotsky," he said.

So I shook my head. "That was Karl's flaw, not mine. Me, I'd be perfectly happy using an axe to swat a fly. Long as I didn't care about whoever the fly was sitting on."

I remember something from a Steve Stills song about paranoia striking deep, and it was all I could do not to smile in the special sort of insulting way that I once practiced in front of a mirror. Bren had misread the situation; he was looking at Kethol, Pirojil, and Durine as though they were my henchmen, ready to take him on.

It would be so easy. He was half-ready to make a final stand against the four of us, and he was good enough—hell, anybody's good enough—that none of the three of them would try for a disarm if he went for his weapons. Just cut him down, fast, and discuss it later.

All I had to do was make a tiny move that let him think I was going for a sword, or a gun. Just drop the right shoulder an inch or two and glance to the left, then jump back as though startled and let Kethol and—

No.

It was all wrong. It could happen too easily—anybody can start a fight, but it's not easy to stop until somebody's lying dead on the ground—but it was all wrong. I was letting my own irritation get in the way.

It didn't matter that while Kirah shuddered at my touch, the night too often brought her groans of orgasm down the halls from where he shared her bed. It didn't matter that he had fallen into my bed and much of my life comfortably while I was away, out on the road saving the goddamn world. That was no reason to trigger a fight. It was every reason *not* to trigger a fight. I might have lost my wife to him, but in ten years, maybe less, it wouldn't rip my guts out, it wouldn't make me want to dig my nails into my palms until they bled. So I really didn't want to see him dead on the ground, his neck bent impossibly to one side, his tongue bulging and black in his mouth, the raw stink of death harsh in my nostrils.

If you keep telling yourself something, you can make it true, but, damn, it's a lousy day when you don't even want your wife's lover dead.

So I held up a hand. "Ta havath, eh? Peace. Let's take a walk, just you and me."

Bren's lips pursed. "My pleasure."

Kethol's mouth twisted into a frown. "I don't much like this."

Pirojil shook his head. "Me, neither. But we'll search the both of them, and then let them do it. Durine?"

The big man nodded. "That ought to do."

* * *

I would have felt a lot more comfortable without-clothes naked than without-weapons naked. Hell, it had been all that I could do to slip one of my throwing knives into the back of Durine's belt while he searched me, then take it back as he turned. If the others had been watching him instead of Bren and me, I never would have been able to pull it off.

We walked in silence for a while between the rows of young trees, until a rise put us out of sight and sound of the others—orchards can easily grow on ground much steeper than you'd like to plow.

He stroked his well-trimmed beard into place. Too damn pretty, and too damn prissy—that was the trouble with the young baron. Or maybe it was that he was too damn young; I was feeling awfully old of late.

"I hear that you're planning on going out again in a few tendays," he said.

I nodded. "A while. No rush." No rush except the dreams, and I wasn't going to be stampeded by my own subconscious. Andy was coming along fast—too fast, in a lot of ways—and she had the level head you expect from a woman in her thirties, but until recently, she hadn't been out on the road for many years, and never without magic to back her up.

"I assume you're going after Jason and Ahira?"

"You'd wish that on me, wouldn't you?" I

snorted. "Like hell." Sure, just what I needed to do with a green partner: help chase down one of our own, somebody who had gone rogue, turned into a serial killer. I mean, this business is likely enough to get you killed when you're acting sensibly; there's no sense in rushing things.

"No," I said, "we're going to hit Home, and pick up some weaponry, and then just pull a snoop around, say, Wehnest."

Who knows what we might learn? I was sure that Lou had spies—excuse me: investigatory representatives—out, but it wouldn't hurt to supplement them. More important, it would give Andrea a taste of what it was like without sticking both our necks in a buzzsaw. If it was necessary to go after Jason and the dwarf, I'd do it myself.

Mainly, though, I wanted to get around and see things. The leakage from Faerie had been plugged—I happened to be there at the time, and even played a small part—but magic and the magical had been leaking out ever faster before that. One of the fringes of this business is that you get to get out and see things, even if too often the things are interested in killing you. It pays to be able to run real fast.

Or to be able to change the subject. "What I'm curious about is what your plans are, Baron."

He didn't answer for a moment as he pulled a small twig from his belt, stripped off the bark with swift movements, and used the point to clean under his fingernails. "That would depend, I guess, on what the ladies want." He eyed me levelly. "I wouldn't be . . . entirely averse to pretending that the last while simply didn't happen, and going back to the way things were: Aeia and me . . . intended; you with your wife, to work out your own problems."

"Really head over heels for Kirah, eh?" If he had made just one move, I would have opened him from guzzle to zorch, and never mind that I'm not exactly sure where the guzzle or zorch is; I'd have kept cutting until I found one.

"What has happened between Kirah and myself is between Kirah and myself. What my feelings are for Aeia are my own," he said, his voice strangely mild, as though he was trying to sound calmer than he was and was overcompensating. "I'm a political realist, Walter Slovotsky, and I'm also Baron Adahan. It's clear to me that a marriage between me and the Cullinane family is of rather greater benefit to the barony than marriage to Kirah would be." He raised a hand. "You're free to make decisions on more personal grounds. I have to think of my people. That aside, I intend no criticism of you, honestly, Walter Slovotsky. What has gone wrong between you and Kirah probably couldn't be helped."

*No, Walter, I'm not being critical of you just be-*

*cause your wife screams when you touch her, you insensitive bastard.*

But it wasn't my fault, and whatever my feelings were for Kirah, I wasn't going to live my life in penance for how others had treated her before I came along. Nor for the fact that the first time we made love was hours after Karl and I had freed her from slavers. She had a choice, dammit. I would have taken a no.

But the back of my mind whispered: *she didn't know that, now did she?*

He held out his hand. "I doubt that we'll ever find a permanent arrangement that suits all of us, but in the interim I suggest a temporary one, just for you and me."

"Oh?"

"Truce," he said, extending a hand. "And more than a truce. I'll cover your back—I'll go out on the road with you and Andrea." He shrugged. "I've been absent enough from my barony; Ranella runs things just fine without me. Until then, nobody will see anything that's not rubbed in his face, eh?"

*But can I trust you, Bren Adahan?*

"It would have to be understood that I'd be in charge on the road," I said. It's one thing to let Ahira call the shots, and another thing entirely to trust somebody who would be better off with me dead.

He nodded. "I believe the phrase is that if you

ask me to jump, I inquire as to how high on the way up?"

"I like it better that when I tell you to take a shit, you squat and ask 'What color?', but you've got the idea."

"It's understood, Walter Slovotsky—I understand that command can't be divided, and that somebody has to be in charge."

Whether I meant it or not, the right thing to do was to say, "You've got a deal, Baron." It could be fixed later. He could be fixed later.

So I did the right thing.

His smile was perhaps a millimeter too wide, and I didn't like it. It said that he was thinking two moves ahead of me, which was entirely possible, given that I didn't know what my next move was. I couldn't see putting things back together with Kirah, I just couldn't, not if that meant giving up Aeia. I had come home determined to do just that, but the combination of finding Bren in Kirah's bed and finding Aeia warming not just my bed but my life had turned that resolve into dust and ashes.

Life gets too goddamn complicated.

We had started to walk back toward the others when Adahan snorted.

"Some things, Walter Slovotsky, should be a lot simpler," he said.

I smiled. I could simplify things with a quick knife move, but I'd already given that up and really didn't consider it. I wouldn't mind stabbing an unarmed man, not if that was the right thing to do, but it wasn't, and that was that.

"I know," I said.

He reached up and cut a sprig from a tree overhead.

Cut?

His smile broadened as he slipped the knife back into his waistband. "It's too bad I won't stab an unarmed man."

I forced myself to nod and shrug. "You've got a point."

I met Andrea Cullinane down in the fencing studio just at noon, as usual.

She was dressed only in a tight cotton halter incongruously above a pair of bulky drawstring pantaloons. The tight halter plumped up her breasts, which didn't particularly need it, leaving her long midriff bare almost to her hips, where the bulky pantaloons concealed the long legs that I had reason to remember with some affection.

"Good ride this morning?"

She smiled. "Good enough. But don't think I'm too tired to move on to the next item on the agenda."

"Wouldn't think of it."

Her long black hair was pulled back tight into a ponytail, which made her ears seem to stick out a trifle, kind of pixieish.

Well, maybe it wasn't incongruous, after all; the purpose of the halter wasn't to make her look great—although it did. Jouncing up and down wasn't likely to do her breasts any good, and while it was amazing what subtle damage a good healing cleric could correct, it was also a bad idea to count on it.

There's a kind of beauty a woman gets as she moves into her late thirties and early forties, if she's lucky. It's not the same thing as the prettiness of a girl in her late teens and twenties, where youthful energy mixes with a sort of pneumatic dynamism that's all fresh and bubbly, even if a bit raw at the edges.

No, there's something else that happens for that period of time between when the baby fat disappears and when the wrinkles take over, when something I think of as balance can make her sexy as all hell. I can't remember a lot of Playboy Playmates in their forties, so I guess it doesn't show up as well on film as it does in the flesh, but Andy had been pretty when I first met her, and was getting more beautiful every year.

Which wasn't something it was a great idea for me to be thinking about the mother—adopted or otherwise—of Aeia.

I stripped off my shirt and tossed it into a corner.

Andy smiled knowingly as she reached for a

pair of practice swords. She tossed one to me, flipping it end-over-end.

"Protect yourself, Walter," she said.

I had to lunge back a half step to catch the sword by the hilt, and by then she was almost on me, her lunge a classic extension from left ankle to right wrist. A sensible man would have been too busy defending himself to notice how sexy she looked that way, but I've never been accused of being sensible.

Oversexed, maybe, but not sensible.

I slapped the blade to one side with the flat of my left hand while I settled the hilt into my right, then swung at her arm with my own practice sword.

Needless to say, her arm wasn't there anymore. The full lunge forward had been followed by a classic recover that brought her out of range and back to a nice en garde position.

I tried a double-feint lunging attack, and only had to hold back a trifle to let her beat it aside.

She was picking this stuff up fast. I said as much.

"Ten years of dance class, Walter," she said, as she tried another attack. "A bit of jazz, and my ballet teacher managed to get me up on toe after less than a year—" she emphasized the last word with a very pretty disengage and lunge.

My built-in skills and almost twenty years of practice were enough to keep her attack at bay, although she did manage to back me up almost all the way across the room. I saw her eyes widen as we approached the balance beam, and could almost see the picture in her mind of me falling ass-backward. Never one to let it be said that Walter Slovotsky would let a lady down, I let my right heel bump into it, then threw up my hands as though fighting for balance.

She was still too green, although it was a close call—but with my hands that high, I was exposed for a thigh wound at the very least, and she should have gone for it. If you can get a disabler, take it; going in for the kill can wait.

But she was still new at this: instead, she took a step forward, waiting for an even better opportunity as I fought for balance or fell.

I whipped my sword down, hard, slashing against her free arm even harder, then fell into a fighting crouch as she turned to bring the hurt arm away from me, and caught her sword hand with the tip of my practice blade hard enough to make her drop her sword.

Give her credit: she didn't scream, but just grunted as the sword fell from her fingers.

I didn't drop my own blade. The lesson wasn't over. "Don't take anything for granted, Andy. Pretending to be hurt, to lose balance, to have a phony tell on an attack—it's all part of the standard repertoire." I wouldn't give her half a chance in a real fight against a real swordsman—except for the surprise factor. Which might be enough. And another few months of this, and who knows? She was talented, and dedicated, and that counts for a lot.

She raised her hands, clasping her fingers behind her neck. "Point taken, sir. I surrender."

That made me mad. "In the field, you know what that means as well as I do. You can't ever afford to lose, or—"

"Or?" The corners of her mouth lifted, and she did something behind her neck with the ties of her halter, and it fell free as she took a step forward, her breasts bobbling free as she gently pushed my sword arm aside and came into my arms. "Or what?" she whispered, her breath warm on my neck.

I started to push her away—"Andy, this isn't a good idea," I started to say—when I felt something sharp and cold prickling at the back of my neck.

She wasn't smiling anymore. "I'm sorry, but I don't have a practice knife—I guess the real thing will have to do. Drop the sword, Walter."

Her smile was broad, but it wasn't pleasant. Think of a lion smiling at a lamb. "If this was for real, I wouldn't have given you that chance." Gentle fingers rested on my second and third rib; a less gentle one poked at the flesh between them. "I would have stuck it here, real, *real* hard," she said, her voice all honeyed and breathy.

As my swordhilt thudded on the floor, she added: "And twisted."

I tried to look mad, but the truth is that I was proud of her.

# 4

## In Which Dinner Is Interrupted

There is a simple, guaranteed way that any woman can make herself look more beautiful to you. More effective than the most expensive of carefully applied cosmetics, more than surgery, than exercise, or hairstyle, or any combination of the above.

It's simple: she can leave you for another man.

—WALTER SLOVOTSKY

The dream is always the same:

*We're trying to make our escape from Hell, millions of us streaming down the endless rows of gym lockers, past the searing lava showers, toward the glowing Open sign, and safety.*

*There's too many of us, of course; I'm on the outside of the crowd, and I keep banging my shin against the locker-room benches, picking up as many bruises as splinters. Once we made it to This Side, I would have bet that there wasn't a chance*

*in hell I'd spend time in a gym again, but, shit, we
are in Hell, eh?*

*Behind us, the demons come. Some are clouds of
acid fog that can eat through a body so fast it will
only scream for an eon as it dissolves; others are
huge wolves, or curiously mutated cats, their ears
long and tufted, their fangs long and yellow. There's
one that looks like a pus-covered Pillsbury Dough-
boy, but there's nothing at all funny about him.*

*They're all chasing us, and they're all getting
closer, and we're not all going to escape.*

*"We'll hold them here," Karl Cullinane shouts.
"Who stands with me?"*

*The crowd rushes away, leaving some of us be-
hind.*

*The old man in the ill-fitting British private's
uniform puzzles me for a moment—he's too old to
be a private soldier—until I hear Eleanor Roosevelt, wrinkled and homely in that comforting way,
call him by name and invite him to stand beside
her, and then I know it's Colonel Meinertzhagen,
slipping out for yet another battle.*

*A short, slim old man, his eyes nearsighted and
in a permanent squint from too many years of ex-
amining things too closely, his fingers not quite
trembling with age, smiles and gives a shrug as he
stoops to send his three grandchildren running toward the exit, then tosses his black bag to one side
and steps forward to link arms with the old Roman
general.*

The general stands himself up straight and murmurs something that I know is old, vulgar Latin—his words end in "-o" where I think there should be an "-us"—but that in the clarity you get only in a dream I know means "It's an honor to stand with you, Doctor."

"Why, General?" he says, his voice thin and reedy. "Wouldn't you have come out of retirement to take care of your grandchildren, if they needed you?"

I don't hear the beginning of the Roman's answer, just "—honors appropriate to the honored."

"I never had any children," another old man says, stepping forward to take the doctor's other arm, "and never even made lieutenant commander, much less flag rank." Under a short brush mustache his smile is not entirely friendly but completely reassuring. He holds his back too straight, beyond that which you expect from a fencer, and maybe that's because he's always been a stiff-necked old bastard, with every bit as much stubbornness as insight—but that's his virtue, not his flaw, and even in a dream I wouldn't change a hair on his permanently balding head any more than I'd dare to change a word he'd written. "But I don't believe they can invalid me out of this one," he says, accepting Cincinnatus' nod as his due.

He is there again, past the old withered form of Tennetty, past Karl Cullinane, still strong and powerful in his old age: the leader of the band of sailors, his beard white as milk.

"Though much is taken, much abides," he says. "Younger, I would have tricked them into following me away, and lured them to their doom," he says. "Younger, I would have tried to trade wit for blood. But today, I shall stand with you, and we will hold them, I swear we will." This time the voice is too harsh, as though he had once ruined it, screaming until he'd hurt himself, and there are scars on his powerful arms. Strong arms and shoulders—well-developed as though he was an oarsman, perhaps? Or an archer? There's another scar above his knee, and I know that means something, but what?

There's something in his manner that tells of a habit of command, and his eyes see too far.

Karl just claps a hand to his shoulder. His voice cracks around the edges, not with fear, but with age. "We will hold them," Karl says. "Who else is with me?"

Then I wake up.

I took my time putting on a fresh white ruffled shirt, black linen trousers pegged nicely at the knee, and a short cape thrown carelessly over my left shoulder—neatly covering the open neck that not only revealed my manly chest but also gave me easy access to the flat knife strapped just below my left armpit—added a few other weapons here and there, and made my way downstairs.

Kirah was already down in the Great Hall of Castle Cullinane. She had dressed for dinner in a black velvet gown that set off her blonde hair and light skin wonderfully in the firelight. She had been spending daylight hours inside of late, it seemed; the light sprinkling of freckles I remembered from the old days was gone from her creamy shoulders.

She made me feel all clumsy, and I didn't much like that. "Hi there," I said, wondering where to put my hands. Damn trousers didn't have pockets, but even that would have been clumsy.

I never used to wonder where to put my hands when I was with Kirah.

She smiled briefly, gently. "Good evening, Walter. Did you have a good day?"

"About like usual. Doranne going to join us at dinner?"

She shook her head. "She had a long day in the stables," she said, with just a trace of disapproval in the way she pursed her lips for a moment before a barely visible shrug dismissed the matter. "I put her to bed."

I nodded. "Important to get enough sleep at that age."

"Yes, it is."

I would have said something else equally awkward and stilted so she could have responded with something about as clumsy, but silence seemed to fill the gap just about as well, so I didn't say anything for a few moments, and then

two of the serving-girls came through the dark
hallway from the kitchen and bustled around the
table, filling water mugs and setting out a carafe
or two of undoubtedly too-young wine, which
filled the silence for yet another moment.

I was starting to say something when Bren
Adahan arrived, a light cape covering a lambskin
jacket and trousers of a sufficiently creamy white
that I would have liked to see the kitchen serving
a particularly messy black-bean-sauce dish.

He briefly nodded to me, removed his cape,
and folded it neatly over the back of the chair,
following it with his swordbelt before he sat
down at the table, adjusting the cuffs of his almost glowingly white shirt.

Kirah gave me an empty smile as she took her
seat down the table on the other side, next to
him.

Aeia came down in a blouse and skirt, the
blouse frilled along a neckline that looked just
this side of dangerously scooped, and the skirt a
floor-length one of raw Kiarian silk that didn't
quite cling to her legs. Her hair was back and up
in some sort of bun that didn't manage to look se-
vere.

But the whole effect was kind of strange; it
was like a little girl playing dress-up. Which was
ridiculous. She was an adult woman, into her
twenties but not thirties, and hadn't been a little
girl, well, as long as I'd known her.

"Good evening," she said, more as a general announcement than any specific wish, and then took her seat next to me.

Janie dashed in, her hair wet from a quick bath, her mannish trousers and shirt far too informal for dinner as she flopped down into place across the table from me, an empty seat between her and Bren Adahan. "Evening, Mom, Dad, Bren, Ay," she said, grabbing up a handful of sweetmeats from the tasting platter that U'len had no doubt deliberately left nearer her place than anybody else's. No, the chief cook doesn't serve in most castles, but U'len was more of an old family retainer than a chief cook, and would no more have let anybody else brown the beef bones for her stock than she would have let some stranger serve Aeia or her mother their food.

Doria appeared at the door, one soldier at her heels, another—Egri, if I remembered right; he was part of the old staff, and the sometimes captain of the guard—at her elbow. She gave him a few whispered parting instructions and made her way to her seat.

Doria, Andrea, Aeia, and Kirah. I was uncomfortable for a moment, but then it reminded me of an old joke: Fred and Bill are at Fred's wedding; Bill's the best man. There are lots of couples dancing, when Fred leans over to Bill and says, "You know, except for my mom, my sister, and my bride, I've slept with every woman in this room."

Bill smiles. "Hey, then, between the two of us, we've had them all."

Well, maybe it wasn't all that funny, after all.

The first course was a clear soup with bits of crunchy greens floating in it, above a half dozen of U'len's translucent, almost transparent, dumplings, thin layers of egg noodle filled with little pieces of wild mushrooms and crispy slivers of spicy West Holtun ham. I still couldn't decide what the secret of the broth was. Normally, I would have tried to charm or lightly bully it out of U'len, and the fat old woman would have enjoyed frustrating me at every conversational turn, but today I just didn't bother. She wouldn't have told me, and I was getting permanently tired of butting my head against walls, even softly.

The conversation at table neatly avoided important subjects, and was chewing its way around to developments in Little Pittsburgh, over in Barony Adahan. I didn't pay much attention, to tell the truth. Little P was smoky and sooty, and while it was turning out the best iron this side of Nehera's kiln, it was doing so in good hands, and that meant it wasn't anybody's problem, not even mine.

U'len had just served up the roast joint of mutton—the secret with mature lamb is always in the marinade, and U'len had one based on

wine and garlic that drew all the gamy taste out
of the meat without destroying its character—
when the quiet of dinner conversation was interrupted by loud sounds from outside the door.

Doria was on her feet and stalking toward the
door before I could say anything, not that she
would have listened.

Right about then, it would have been handy to
have Karl or Tennetty or Ahira or even Jason at
my side, but Karl and Tennetty were dead, and
the other two were far away.

Naked doesn't mean the same thing as un-
clothed. It means unprotected; it means there's
maybe a problem and there's nobody who you
want at your back—well, at your back.

But you deal with the problem anyway. Shit.

I would have made some comment about how
there were always interruptions when I was enjoying my dinner, but truth to tell I had, unchar-
acteristically, eaten several bites of mutton
without even noticing how it tasted, so I dropped
my eating prong, pulled a brace of pistols from
their hidden pockets in my cape, and offered one
to Adahan butt-first as he rose from his chair. I
mean, I didn't really think we were going to have
to fight our way out, but the help in a well-run
castle don't have loud conversations outside the
Hall during mealtime, not unless there's trouble,
and I've killed at least four people I didn't really
think I was going to have to.

So I don't much care what I don't really think.

His smile and headshake were condescending as he tucked one of his own pistols in the back of his belt, buckling his swordbelt around him as he followed me.

Trouble was standing in the entry foyer, in the persons of three men in black and silver Imperial livery facing off against Durine, who was blocking their way into the castle, his hands neither terribly close to nor terribly far from the pistols and sword at his belt.

I took an instant dislike to the Imperial captain—he had the sort of over-cared-for skinny mustache that I always associate with Simon Legree and my junior-year English teacher. I've always figured that somebody who has enough time to spend on diddling with a mustache ought to get a real hobby.

"What's the problem, Durine?" Doria asked.

"The problem—" the captain started.

"She asked Durine, not you," Bren Adahan put in, saving me the trouble.

"And who would you be?" the captain asked, his lip curled two degrees past insolent.

"She's Doria Perlstein, baronial regent. And I'm Bren Adahan," he said. "_Baron_ Adahan."

It really was almost as good as pulling Marshall McLuhan out from behind a billboard—better, in context.

The captain's sneer melted into a stiff mask,

and the tips of his ears were red as he gave a short, stiff-necked bow. "My apologies, Baron," he said, producing a folded piece of parchment from his belt pouch. "But I am on a mission from the Emperor, and my warrant requires that all Imperial subjects give me 'aid, assistance, help, and succor' in my mission." He tapped a fingernail on the paper. "It's signed by the Emperor himself."

"And you showed it to Durine?" Doria asked.

Durine shrugged. "I don't read much."

She glared at him. I would have told her that she'd missed the point, but it wasn't the time and place. You can't just order the likes of Durine and his friends around, not by flashing a set of credentials. There's nothing worse that the likes of the captain could do than have them killed, and they've stared that in the face more than a few times, and long since worked out that they're not going to live forever. It might scare them—hell, it does scare them, every single time—but they can't afford to give a damn about how scared they are. If they let that stop them once, just once, it's all over.

The captain had rubbed him the wrong way, and it would take more than an Imperial writ to get him to back down.

You deal with men like that straightforwardly, on their terms. I stared at Durine until he returned the look, for just a moment. I held his gaze with mine, then nodded fractionally, then raised my open palm slightly, for just a second, punctuating the motion with a shrug. *I understand, and you did fine; take it easy—I'll handle things.*

For a moment, it could have gone either way. But then he nodded.

Bren Adahan was smiling behind his hand. *Nicely done,* his smile said.

The captain was still talking to Doria. ". . . case," he said, "now that I've established my credentials, may I have your cooperation?"

"That would depend, I suppose," Doria said, "on what it is that you want."

The captain nodded. "Just the baron—Baron Jason Cullinane, that is. The Emperor requires his presence at the capital."

"Well, he isn't here," I put in. "And what do you want him for?"

"I don't have authorization to discuss that." The captain produced another sheet of parchment. "Then I'm told to use my judgment and bring along anybody else who might be of use. I judge that to consist of you, the baron—"

"—and me," Andy put in, walking up from behind me. "Captain Mastishch."

He did a double take, and then bowed. "Of course, your Highness." Never mind that Andrea wasn't the wife of his Prince and Emperor—Karl was dead—or the mother of the Heir and therefore Dowager Empress, she was close enough to being royalty for Captain Mustache, or Mastish, or whatever his name was.

"And me, too," Aeia put in, from behind her adopted mother.

Well, there was one thing to be said for being arrested. It was a fine interruption in a less-than-tranquil home life, and I wasn't likely to be sleeping alone.

"We leave in the morning," he said. He turned to Doria. "In the name of the Emperor, I will require shelter and food for my horses and men."

"Will he bother to tell the difference?" I muttered.

Bren Adahan didn't bother to hide that smile behind his hand.

I turned and went back to dinner, not inviting Mastishch along.

Of course, Doria did, which ruined both the whole effect and the rest of the meal.

Clearing her hair from her eyes with a toss of her head, Aeia turned over in bed and tried to burrow under the covers. Sheets were tangled about her waist, almost as though she'd wound them like a sarong.

I reached out and ran a hand down her side, stopping at her hip, pulling her gently toward me.

Her eyes opened. "You *are* awake," she said, turning, her breath warm in my ear.

"Just a little." Better to be awake than to dream. I was dreaming too much, and it was all too confusing.

She rested her head on the crook of my elbow, her eyes searching mine. For what, I don't know, although maybe she did: the tenseness in her body eased.

"It's not that bad, Walter," she said. "Just a trip to Biemestren."

"Just a summons to Biemestren. Three days on the road, with little enough privacy."

She laughed. "Is that what you're worried about? Walter, they've rebuilt most of the Prince's Inns. We'll sleep in clean beds, in a room with a thick door—" she caught herself. "Very nicely done, sir."

"Eh?"

"A nice attempt to distract me, to make me think that what's bothering you is not having enough time alone with me."

I dialed for a smile. "That fear is enough to make a satisfied man hunger in advance, to make a brave man tremble, to—"

"Too prettily put," she said, drawing a sheet around her as she sat up in bed. I admired the strategy; the last time she had tried to push me on this, I had distracted her by reaching for her. "But that's not what's bothering you." A long finger gently stroked my arm from shoulder to wrist;

her fingers snaked in among mine, then clutched my hand firmly. "What is?"

I shrugged. "Fears. Dreams. Nightmares. I'm afraid of going out again. I'm getting too old for this. I could get somebody hurt, or worse."

There was more to it than that. The dreams had changed, but they were always the same, and the effect was the same. I was going out not because I was brave or anything, but because I was afraid of my own nightmares. Not because some friends might need me, not because there was, the way the man in my dream said, some work of noble note, but because I couldn't bear to face my own nightmares.

There're times when I'm not very proud of myself.

"You don't have to go out again," she said. "Not alone."

"No," I said.

"Walter—"

"*No*. I won't take you with me. I will not have you die in my arms on some dirty road somewhere. I won't see you torn to bits by some inhuman thing; I won't watch you blown to bits of bloody, stinking flesh." I started to choke. "I won't do it. I've done it with too many people I love, and I'm not going to do it with you." Karl, Tennetty, the lot of them—and now Andy wanted to come on the road with me.

Okay; so be it. I had promised.

But not Aeia. She would stay safe, regardless, even if that meant the end of us. I couldn't—

She touched a fingertip to my lips.

"Shhh. I said I'll wait for you," she whispered, her cheek warm and wet against mine. "I'll always wait for you."

I pulled the sheet away from her and pulled her close.

Her lips were salty with tears, although I couldn't have told you whose they were.


The last thing I did before leaving was to say goodbye to my wife and daughters, although not quite in that order.

It wasn't even my intention. I mean, I couldn't think of anything that needed saying between Kirah and me.

Janie and Doranne were down in the stables, playing with the horses.

Doranne was dressed in her usual play outfit— grayed cotton top and drawstring trousers over brand new leather boots (if I wasn't a rich man, putting new shoes on my younger daughter would break me quickly)—and Janie was in her riding togs, but with a difference: an overjacket that I hadn't seen before, covered with about half a dozen pockets, varying in size from a thumb-sized one that probably held a small sharpening stone to a big square one that could have held a large lunch. It looked sort of like an Other Side photographer's vest, except with sleeves.

"Nice," I said, as she tucked a withered carrot from the vegetable bin into one of the larger pockets. "New?"

"Mother," she said.

"Yes, Daddy," Doranne said. "Mommy made it for her. Says when I'm old enough to go riding, she'll make me one."

It had a loose fit to it; I patted at the left side, feeling a hard bulge underneath. Ah.

Her smile broadened. "A going-away present from my boyfriend. I figured to keep it on me while you're gone."

"You expecting trouble, sweetness?"

Her shrug was casual. "Not really, but without my Daddy here to protect me, I figured that I'd better keep something handy, particularly if I'm going to go riding often."

"But not at any regular time. You can—"

"Really, Dad, I'm not Doranne." She patted my arm. "I'll be good."

Regular habits are an assassin's or kidnapper's dream, particularly regular habits that involve things like going for a ride. We did the best we could—the local village wardens had their ears and eyes out for strangers—but there's no sense in giving the other guy any edge at all.

I sighed. Back in Endell, my family was surrounded by a whole dwarf nation, fully protected on the occasions that I had left them. A keep in the Middle Lands, even one as well built and well run as the hereditary Furnael keep that was now Castle Cullinane, just wasn't the same, and I didn't like it much.

On the other hand, if I had any real reason to worry, I could pack them off with Ellegon for Home or Endell, the next time the dragon came through. That was only a little more than a week off, if he kept to his regular schedule.

I brought up the subject.

Janie shook her head. "No, I don't think so, Daddy. You might be able to talk me into coming along to Biemestren, but not going away from Holtun-Bieme."

"Oh?"

She looked me in the eye. "Jason asked me to wait for him, before he left. I said I would." The words were casual, but her voice wasn't.

My first thought was that they were both too young, by half, and my second thought was that I didn't want my daughter married off to another suicidal Cullinane, and my third thought was that whatever my thoughts were, I'd best keep them to myself, so I did.

Janie smiled. "Such self-control." She reached up and patted my cheek. "Now give us a hug and kiss goodbye, and then go say goodbye to Mom."

"Yes, dear." I picked up Doranne and held her close for a moment. It would have been longer, but there were horses to play with, and, after all, I was just her father.

It was a first for me: I knocked on the door to Kirah's bedroom.

Husbands and wives should allow each other some privacy, but for us her private place had always been her sewing room, whether the tiny, southern-exposed room in the Old House, or the little cell off our suite in the Endell warrens—but never our bedroom.

Then again, it wasn't our bedroom, not anymore.

"Come in," she said, her voice muffled by the thick door.

Her eyes widened for a moment when the door opened. She was curled up in a chair, working at some knitting or tatting or whatever, and after a momentary hesitation, the long steel needles clicked and clacked in the mound of dark yarn on her lap.

I took a step toward her—

*—sweeping her up in my arms, the knitting or tatting or whatever the hell the damn stuff was falling to one side, ignored by the both of us as I held her close, both tightly and gently, my fingers playing with the small, fine hairs at the base of her neck, hidden under the shower of golden hair, her arms fastening almost painfully hard around me, her warm lips murmuring over and over again, I'm sorry,*

_Walter, please hold me, I'm sorry, Walter, please hold me, I'm sorry, Walter, please hold me . . ._

—and stopped myself. "I thought I should stop by and say goodbye. We'll be on the road within the hour."

There was no anger in her eyes, on her face, no hate. Nothing, except perhaps a residual tenderness that hurt more than I thought such a mild emotion could hurt.

"Goodbye, then," she said.

"I guess I should send Bren up to say goodbye."

Her smile was two degrees this side of cold. "I'm sure that won't be necessary, Walter, but thank you."

I shut the door gently behind me; it was all I could do not to try to yank it off its hinges.

But all I would have done was hurt my shoulder and hand.

# 5

## "Welcome to Biemestren"

It's easier to get forgiveness than to get permission.

—WALTER SLOVOTSKY

Stash's—Dad's—best friend was always Big Mike Warcinsky, two hundred and fifty pounds of huge-footed, blue-suited cop, the sort of guy who at best never looked quite right in civilian clothes. He could never be bothered to match colors or patterns, and since he always wore one of his fourteen working pairs of black size-thirteen Corcoran walking shoes—"Change your shoes and socks halfway through the day, kiddo, and your feet can take you as far as you wanna go"—and knee-height black support socks, he looked amazingly silly in an aloha shirt and plaid shorts, what with his legs that looked like hairy sausages, and the way his open shirt revealed fishbelly-white flesh below his well-tanned face and neck.

He was funny to watch over the barbeque in the backyard, working the long-handled spatula and fork, or at the head of the table on Thanksgiving, getting ready to carve the ham—that was, for years, the family tradition for holidays.

I learned something from that funny-looking man on the Weekend of the Two Turkeys, although it took some years to sink in. I should have already learned part of it the time we went fishing on Lake Bemidji, but I'm slow sometimes.

I guess I must have been about six or seven. The first turkey was the first one that Emma had ever made—my brother Steve had finally nagged her into it, because all the other kids' families had turkeys on Thanksgiving, and Steve didn't learn not to give a shit about what all the other kids' families did until after he left for Vietnam.

What Mom didn't know, because she'd never made a turkey before, is that the people who packed the turkey put the giblets package in the fold of flesh at the front of the turkey, where the neck used to be, and not in the body cavity, like they do with chickens.

Well, she cooked the turkey with the paper

packet in place, and when Big Mike stood up to the head of the table to carve the bird—Stash never liked handling knives when he could find somebody else to do it—the first thing Big Mike naturally did was to cut open the little bump at the front, where clever cooks hide a bit of extra stuffing to become all crispy on the outside.

Big Mike was in the middle of a story—something improbable about how he'd gotten a local pimp to leave town—as he started carving, and out popped this scorched packet of paper.

It all became very clear to Mom, whose jaw dropped.

Without a missing a beat, he flipped it aside and put his carving knife to work on the drumstick, and carved that turkey down to the bone, never once referring to or even looking at the burnt lump of paper. It had ceased to exist for him.

The second turkey appeared that Sunday, when Big Mike. came over for our post-Thanksgiving last cookout of the year—the second turkey was an idiot burglar, who, as it turned out, had been across the alley and down the block at Mrs. O'Keefe's, riffling through her jewelry box, when she came home. Understandably, she had started screaming; surprised, in panic, the scumbag had punched her, trying to shut her up, then fled when she wouldn't stop.

Big Mike and I were out in the backyard when

we heard the scream and the crash of a door and the pounding of feet, and a few seconds later we saw the burglar as he pulled himself up and over the six-foot-high cedar fence that Dad had built to give us a bit of privacy.

Big Mike had been getting ready to start the hamburgers, over by the far corner, while I'd been playing with some toy or another over by the gate.

"Get the fuck out of my way," the burglar shouted, charging for the open gate, toward me. I remember the burglar as being huge, but that's just my memory betraying me, no doubt—he was probably around seventeen, skinny, almost as scared as I was. In retrospect, it was clear he was going to run right over me. He was young and lean and fast, and he was starting off closer to me than Big Mike was, and there was no way that from a standing start, Big Mike could beat him to me.

But there Big Mike was, tangling up the burglar's feet with one clumsy-looking thrust of his long spatula, sending the kid skidding almost chin first on the ground. One quick kick turned him over, leaving the burglar staring at the twin points of a barbeque fork inches away from his eyes, and at the funny-dressed fat man in the support socks and black shoes, who was already shouting to Stash to call in for support—Big Mike used the police code number, but I can't for the life of me remember if it was ten-thirteen, seven-eleven, or sixty-nine.

"Just fucking lie there, turkey," he said, sounding bored. "Just fucking lie there, or I'll put your fucking eyes fucking out." He lifted his head and grinned reassuringly at me. "It's okay, kid. Just go tell your Mom I need another beer, eh?"

Big Mike held him there for a few minutes, until the police arrived and led him away.

It only occurred to me later that the only possible way for Big Mike to have gotten between the burglar and me was if he had started before either of us had ever seen the burglar, if his first reaction at the crashing sounds had been to get close to Stash's kid, because he was the adult on scene, and the first thing you do when it all hits the fan is protect those who need protecting, and to hell with spilled beers.

I've thought about the Weekend of the Two Turkeys from time to time since then. I know there was more at stake with a burglar who might have seriously hurt me than with Mom just having a few moments of embarrassment, so it's real easy to miss that Big Mike was doing the same thing when he blithely ignored that charred, paper-covered lump as he doing when, without warning, without even thinking about it, he lunged forward to be sure he was between me and danger:

It's called being a hero.

\* \* \*

I wonder if the first time that Ugh the caveman was in trouble with Grunt, the leader of the tribe—say, for having bitten off too large a piece from the joint roasting over the fire—Grunt made Ugh worry about how much trouble hc was in by making Ugh wait outside the cave until Grunt was ready to see him.

Hell, it probably goes back before that. I would have asked Jane Goodall, but she wasn't handy.

We had barely settled into our rooms and I had only managed to get the skimpiest of baths to pull days of road dust out of my pores when the summons came for the three of us—Aeia not included.

So I dressed quickly and joined Andy and Bren, and we were escorted toward the throne room, and we waited.

And waited, all the while getting madder, because even if you know exactly what he's doing, the make-them-wait routine is infuriating.

And waited, while I fumed silently and Andy paced.

If anything could have made me madder, it was the way that Bren Adahan idled in a chair, one leg crossed over the other, a half-smile on his face.

And waited until the door swung outward, and old Enrel slowly, painfully hobbled into the room, supporting himself mainly by leaning on massive Hivar on one side and a knobby stick on the other. He was favoring his right side, and from the way he limped it appeared to be his right hip that was going, degenerating. Healing draughts would only relieve the pain and inflammation temporarily, if that was so; the natural state of the bones and ligaments wasn't healthy. A good Spidersect healer could probably keep the pain manageable, but it would take a Hand cleric to teach the bone and muscle to be healthy again, and the Hand women kept clear of the Empire.

Bitches.

Enrel forced himself to straighten, and took a few steps away from Hivar.

Hivar was the after picture to Durine's before: a huge man, now bowed with age, but with still enough strength in his wrinkled hands and enough gleam in his dark eyes that only the very strong or the very foolish would have wanted to arm wrestle him.

He and Hivar stood like a couple of mismatched bookends on either side of the young guards, two old Furnael family retainers who probably weren't up to the job of seeing to the Emperor's needs, but who would go home and die if they were dismissed from his service, no matter what the pretext.

"The Emperor will see you now," Enrel said, his voice strong despite his age.

Two heavily armed guards gave us an appropriate glare as the doors to the throne room swung open.

Everybody has to do things differently, I guess. Holding court was something that Karl did only when he felt he had to, but Thomen had a different idea.

And a different look.

Old.

It took me a moment to remember that the graying man on the raised throne at the end of the long red carpet was actually younger than Aeia—he was still in his early twenties. I needed that self-reminder as I looked at a beard that now was shot with the same gray that touched his receding hairline. His forehead had begun to develop wrinkles, and his shoulders a slouch, and there were crow's feet at the corners of his eyes.

Dr. Slovotsky's diagnosis was overwork, his prognosis was guarded, and his prescription would have been for about three tendays of hard physical labor alternated with good food and drink and long hours of sleep, but I didn't put it forward. For one thing, his mother was there in the throne minor to his left, and she was sure to slap down any suggestion I made.

The years hadn't been kind to Beralyn, and for once I was in sympathy with the years.

Hair that had once been a rich brown had gone gray, and not a silvery, full gray, but a dull and thin one. There were hollows in her cheeks, and her sharp jawline had gone all doughy.

The eyes searched me, and then her gaze swung past, but I knew she was still watching me as she sat curled up inside a cloak that should have been too warm for a room that was well heated against a chilly evening by a man-high fireplace.

The servitor took up a position in front of the throne, then beckoned us forward, stopping us with a raised palm a good ten feet from the throne.

Thomen didn't say anything for too long. His mother just watched me.

I knew why Beralyn hated me—she held Karl responsible for her older son's death, and me for her husband's, and there was some justice in her position—but what the fuck was with Thomen?

The back of my neck itched, and it felt like there was a painful hole to my left where Ahira should have been. We had been relieved of our firearms and my throwing knives—well, the ones they'd found; I wasn't quite naked—but had been allowed to keep our swords, in keeping with our positions: in Bren's case, as a baron of a fully invested barony; in Andrea's, as the other woman who was technically the Dowager Empress; and in my case, because of what a swell guy I am, I supposed.

That had made me feel better; but what didn't

make me feel better were the arrow loops high in the wall beyond and behind the throne. For a pair of archers or gunners in the guardroom beyond, the combined beaten-fire area covered the room, except for a roughly triangular area surrounding the throne. Karl had had the arrow loops plugged during his tenure, but the plugs were gone and we were being watched too carefully from behind the darkened curves.

Finally, the Emperor spoke. "Thank you for coming," he said, the chill in his voice making the words purely pro forma. "I don't see Baron Cullinane."

I should have simply let it slide; after all, if he didn't know that Jason hadn't accompanied us, his staff work left more than a lot to be desired.

But my mouth had its own mind. "Well, maybe if you looked a little harder?" I said, pretending to go through my pockets.

It was a tough room; the audience didn't appreciate it. Thomen just eyed me impassively, while his two old retainers glared and the guards pretended not to have heard. A flicker of a smile crossed his mother's dry lips, but it was one of victory, not amusement.

There was a long silence. "He was not in the barony when your captain came for him," Bren said. "He hasn't returned from a trip yet."

Thomen's lips pursed. "I assume you have a way of sending word to him?"

I shrugged. "Same way you could, I suppose. Ellegon should be through soon, and if you ask him real prettily, he'll probably be willing to add some of the usual rendezvous locations to his stops, what with Jason maybe needing a bit of assistance. The dragon can carry a letter from you just . . ."

*Just as well as it could from anybody else, asshole,* didn't seem to be the right way to put it, even without the epithet. ". . . er, just as well as not."

"That hardly explains why Baron Cullinane is absent from his barony when he's needed there," Dowager Empress Beralyn put in, as though she had been waiting for the opportunity, which seemed more than vaguely likely.

"He left somebody competent in charge," Andrea said, glaring back at her, one Dowager Empress to another. "And I wasn't aware of any requirement that all barons keep their persons within their borders, or even within the borders of Holtun-Bieme," she added, her voice rising ever so slightly in pitch and volume.

Beralyn opened her mouth, then closed it.

Thomen's lips narrowed. "Perhaps there isn't. But there's a matter in Barony Keranahan that needs looking into, and I wanted Jason to do that for me."

I didn't think that called for an answer. Jason was needed in his barony and needed to be out handling problems for Thomen, both at the same time?

Then again, I didn't exactly think that a raised eyebrow was an answer.

"It appears that Baroness Keranahan is trying to force a young noblewoman into a marriage with one of her minor nobles. A marriage of the Baroness' convenience, not the young woman's. Or mine." He smiled thinly.

It was clearly time for Andrea or Bren to speak up and take the heat off me, but they apparently disagreed, so I shrugged. "You should be able to send any of a number of people to handle that sort of thing."

I mean, sure, it would take more authority than Thomen would typically hand to one of his proctors, but not much else. Somebody with a few brain cells to click together, and maybe a good hand or two with a sword and gun in case things got less tricky and more blunt, but that was about all. Hardly necessary to weigh in with the Cullinane name and legend, and probably not a good idea; you don't want to use your legendary heroes too often, for fear of using up either their legend or the heroes. "If not, you might try the three mus—I mean, Durine, Kethol, and Pirojil."

"Or perhaps yourself, Walter Slovotsky?" His smile was thin. "Certainly that would not be something beyond your abilities or beneath your dignity."

I tried to smile. "I don't have much dignity, but I do have some other obligations." And no desire at all to be running errands for the Furnael family, not at the moment. Particularly not if it was a minor little problem that Thomen's mother approved of me handling. Likely to be the equivalent of just gargling with a little innocent but undiluted $H_2SO_4$, or having my temperature taken with just a few yards of gently sharpened double-edged sword, or something equally trivial.

"More pressing than doing as I . . . ask?" he asked, his tone of voice lower in a way that was either very deceptive or even more threatening.

Look at it any of three ways. Maybe I needed some time off, in which case, I should be kicking back and spending my days trying to invent the local equivalent of the piña colada, my evenings in conversation with Aeia, and my nights in bed with her.

Or maybe what I needed to be doing was getting Andy and me into shape to go out on the road.

Or maybe I needed to let my bully of a subconscious kick me into getting back on the road to do something important.

None of it reduced down to going out on the road to act as some sort of Dear Abby for Thomen.

"Well, I wouldn't want to put it that way." I raised a hand. "But, please. As a favor to an old family friend: think about it overnight before making a final decision to . . . push the matter."

I could have pointed out that I wasn't technically an Imperial subject—I hadn't been born into their peasant class or sworn a noble oath-of-fealty—but since I was about to ask a favor I didn't think that getting involved in technicalities was a good idea. Or arguing at all with Thomen. He needed the lecture about how to treat your friends and how not to treat them, but he wasn't about to listen to it from me.

Then again, he could have argued that I wasn't really an old family friend, that my association with his father had gotten his father killed. And if he forgot, his mother was there; she would have gladly pointed it out.

"Very well," he said.

"Another thing, if I may?"

Another glare. "Yes?"

"I find myself in need of . . . a divorce from my wife."

"We will discuss that tomorrow." He turned to Bren and Andrea. "You will join me for dinner, please, along with your families." He looked at me, and then at Andrea. "And be sure to bring your daughter, Aeia." He stood, suddenly, wobbling ever so slightly. "You are dismissed."

Without another word, he turned and walked out of the room, his mother and the rest of his retinue following him.

I looked at Bren, and then at Andrea. "Well, since nobody else is going to say it, I will: Welcome to Biemestren."

I don't know who said it first, but when in doubt, I check with an engineer.

The senior engineer on duty downstairs at the dungeon armory was somebody I knew, if casually, from years ago in Home, before we'd gone off in our separate directions. Each to his own, eh?

It's good to see old friends again. The years had added some gray to his receding hairline and barely trimmed beard, and some lines around his eyes, and more than a few inches to his waistline, but at least his frown was still intact. Some things should never change.

"Good evening, Walter Slovotsky; I'll be with you in a moment," he said, raising the finger of his free hand to forestall me, not looking up from his writing desk. He dipped the pen in ink and scratched out a few quick phrases, then frowned at them, crossed them out, and substituted something else, then set his pen down and rose, cleaning his ink-stained hands on a rag before extending one hand to me. The balance and weights had been pushed to one side; most of the desk was taken up with his writing paper.

"Hi, Jayar," I said. "Still working on the history?"

"Sort of," he said, gesturing me to a chair. "Thought I'd do a play, now that theater is opening up in Biemestren again. It's been a while, Walter."

"Since you've seen me, or since there's been theater in Biemestren?"

"Both. You've been a bit busy, I take it." Each of us to our own failings; Jayar couldn't help using the phrase "a bit" too much.

"You wouldn't believe it." I mean, I could have told him about the hole between reality and Faerie that we'd sealed, or about Boioardo, but those were the sorts of things where you had to be there. He might well have believed that I had given away the secret of making black powder, but I didn't see any need to go into that.

He gave one of those all-knowing smiles that I find only barely sufferable when I see it in a mirror. "Perhaps. But since you're not down here to talk over old times, and since you're not going to talk about recent ones, what can I do for you?"

I dropped an almost-empty powderbag on the table. "I'll need some of your best, for a start. And if we're not going to talk over told times or recent ones, how about current events?" I jerked my thumb over my shoulder. "I had an audience with Thomen today."

"And it wasn't all you expected, eh?" He pulled a balance and a set of weights, and then a stone pot, out from a cabinet to his right. He hefted my powderbag. "I've seen cleaner—any real chance your powder got contaminated?"

I shrugged. "Seems unlikely, despite everything. But not impossible."

"Better safe than sorry?" At my nod, he pulled a new-looking bag from the drawer, and carefully weighed out a triple load of powder before looking up and smiling. "Enough for a trip to Barony Keranahan, eh?"

I didn't return his smile. "Rather more than enough for that. I'm a talker, not a fighter."

"That's what I hear." He screwed a brass tip onto the ring inset into the mouth of the bag, then set it down in front of me. "As to the Emperor, you've got to see it from his point of view, at least a bit. While he was regent, he had all the . . . mystique of the Cullinanes to call on, to buttress his authority, and he could have turned it all over to the Heir at any time." Jayar sighed. "These days, he's stuck in a box, and can't be expected to like it much, or to be all that friendly toward those who put him there."

"Like me."

He shrugged. "Like you, or Jason, or Ahira. Or even the dragon." Somehow or other, despite his attempt to keep things all neat and in their place, he had spilled perhaps half a teaspoonful of gunpowder on the desk. He looked at me seriously, soberly as he took a piece of paper and used it to sweep the powder into a stone bowl.

I made the sign of the scales with my hands. "Should I be worried, brother Engineer?" Technically, I'm an engineer—pretty much by Engineer definition, since I know how to make gunpowder, and that's an Engineer secret. Well, it was. I traded the secret for our lives in Brae, but I didn't see that mentioning it to this engineer was likely to earn any plaudits or help.

He sobered. "Not, brother Engineer, if you don't confront him directly. But I would say that his mother holds a deep hatred for you, and I would not give her an excuse to argue to him that you are a threat to his reign, or his dynasty." He picked up the piece of flint from the desk, and stroked it lightly against the side of a metal file, sending a spark into the bowl.

With a loud _whoom,_ the gunpowder flashed into flame and heat that felt like a sudden blush, and then was gone, leaving behind a cloud of smoke and a stink of sulfur.

"Sometimes," he said, "the easiest thing to do with something is to get rid of it."

We had been quartered off in the new wing of the keep, up on the third floor, where the imported Nyphien tapestries showed the usual Nyphien scenes of Nyph soldiers defending villages from the onslaught of hordes of stylized firebreathing dragons, even though, at least until recently, it had been hundreds of years since there had been much of a draconic presence in the Eren regions, much less the Middle Lands.

Magical creatures and humans don't seem to get along—with some exceptions.

Hell, if humans don't get along with other humans—granted, with some exceptions—why should magical creatures be any better at it?

Aeia and I had been assigned rooms at the opposite ends of the long hall, but she hadn't even pretended to settle into hers before putting her things in with me and mine. Stubbornness runs in the Cullinane family, and besides, this had been her father's house before it was Thomen's, and she wasn't about to let him tell her where to sleep.

I wish she had asked me; my digs were small. Her room was a three-room suite, suitable to her station; mine appeared to have been quarters for either a not particularly large upstairs maid or perhaps a more royal agoraphobe.

My room had been furnished so as to not overburden the occupant with luxury: the stone walls were bare of any hanging or tapestry; the furnishings consisted of a small, plain stand, a bedframe, and a duckfeather-filled mattress. A bottle of cheap wine, a loaf of dark bread, and a hunk of unlikely cheese sat on a relatively clean plate on the nightstand.

While Aeia hung a lantern from a hook on the wall, I took my bag from the bed and dropped it to the floor, then dropped to all fours to look under the bed for a moment.

"What are you looking for?" she asked.

"Round-shouldered mice."

She took a moment to work it out, then laughed. I liked that about her. She didn't take my word something was funny, the way Kirah had when we were young, and she never asked for an explanation she didn't need, or failed to ask for one when she did.

"I'm supposed to be down at dinner in a few minutes," she said. "With Thomen, and Bren and Mother. And the other Dowager Empress."

"You won't have to sneak me up anything," I said. "The bread and cheese will do." While I could have eaten over in the barracks with the officers or down in the kitchen with the staff, I had ordered a tray and a bottle of wine sent up to the rooms. Probably not my best move, if I wanted the best Biemestren could offer, but that wasn't one of my higher priorities.

She frowned. "That wasn't what I was asking, and you know better, and I know better, and you know that I know you aren't just appetites at both ends," she said, touching a finger first to my lips, and then, well, just below the belt. "Do you want me to try to find anything out?"

"Nah." I shook my head. "Just listen."

Her lips tightened for a moment, then relaxed. "It isn't that you don't think I'm capable of inquiring without getting into trouble, so it's not that. And it isn't that you think I'm in danger, because you know better, so it's probably that you've got somebody else primed to ask around. Mother?"

I shook my head. "No, it's not that." I tried not to think much about Andy, and for a whole variety of reasons. There was something a bit perverse about sharing a bed with her (adopted, granted) daughter that I didn't like to think about, because there was nothing perverse about sharing my life with Aeia. Which didn't mean I'd share every moment, or every thought with her. I'm not built that way.

Sorry.

One corner of one lip turned up. "Did something . . . happen between you and Mother out on the road? Something you want to tell me about?"

That was an easy question. "No." There was nothing I wanted to talk about. What had happened with Andy and me had been more of a collision than anything else.

Here's a difference: When things were right between us, Kirah would have known enough not to ask any further. She would just have let the matter drop, and turned back to her knitting or something.

"Oh." One corner of Aeia's lip turned up. "Then it's something you don't want to talk about, eh?" And she chuckled. "What was that old saying you used to tell me about? From your actor friend?"

" 'Drunk and on the road don't count.' Old theater saying," I said, deadpan.

She nodded. "So, is there something that I need to know about?" Fingers stronger than they looked entwined with mine.

"That's an interesting question."

"Phrased very carefully, too," she said. "And ready to live with whatever your answer is." She touched a finger to my lips for a moment. "I've known you for a long time."

"Then: no. Nothing happened that you need to know about. Okay?"

"Okay." She laid her head on my chest. "Then that's just fine with me, Walter." I could feel her whole body relax. "The thing is, you see, I trust you. Not to tell me everything—not even to tell me the truth all the time. I just trust you."

Which was exactly the right thing to say. And also it left out the wrong things to say. With the people you really care about, it's not just what they say that matters, but what they don't say, what they know you know them well enough to understand without the words. My left hand may not know what my right hand is doing, but it doesn't need to tell my right hand to watch out for it all the time.

When I had first met Aeia, many, many years ago, she had been a badly beaten, ill-used, scared little girl staggering out of a slaver's wagon. Looking back, I can remember seeing something of character and strength in her eyes, but where did she grow this kind of balance and judgment, and when and how had we become part of each other so?

I could have asked, but I guess I don't have to know everything, either.

Her arms came around my neck. "I should go downstairs for supper shortly. You have any idea how we could spend the time until then?"

I thought about it for a moment, and then I thought about how she'd feel when she found me gone later, how she'd smile and shake her head and say that she should have worked it all out before she'd been left seduced and abandoned, but how she really wouldn't mean it, and then I thought about how firm and insistent her lips felt on mine, how warm and sweet her tongue was in my mouth, and how good her hair smelled and how easily a trained thief's fingers, even an aging thief's fingers, could loosen a button or unhook a belt, and then I thought about how silky smooth her skin was, then how firm and strong and limber the muscles were beneath that silky skin, and then I stopped thinking for a while.

Thinking is, sometimes, vastly overrated.

The wine bottle stood empty, but that was just because I'd taken it down the hall and poured almost all of it down the garderobe, leaving only an inch or so in the glass. Drinking and skulking mix only if you want to get caught.

I'd taken a few moments to memorize the room, and then blown out the lamp. The room was barely lit by the flicker of torches from the inner curtain wall and too much light streaming under the door. I rolled up a thick blanket and laid it down in front of the door, which made me feel for a moment like a college kid. All I needed was a joint and a fan to blow the smoke out the window.

I let my eyes adjust to the dark. Well, it was nice to be here in peacetime: the barred latticework that could have been fastened over the windows had been slid up to the ceiling, although the sockets it would lock into were covered only by the curtains and not blocked even by any furniture. Two brass staples, each about the size of my fist, were embedded in the wall on either side, wooden wedges slipped into them. To slip the wedges out, slide the latticework down into the embedded sockets, then bash the wedges back into place, further locking the latticework down, would take five minutes, max. Less than a day for the staff to switch the keep from peace mode to a wartime siege footing.

I don't know that hoping has ever made something so, but I do it for practice; it just might: I hoped everything was on a relaxed peacetime routine as I set up the washbasin on the battered old dresser next to the window, then blackened my face with a nice water-based gunk I bought from a traveling mummer troupe. When I was finished with it, it matched the mottled color of the dark pants and pullover shirt I'd changed into.

The boots were light, but inside the leather the square toes were metal-capped, and under the toe, between the two layers of the sole, was a concealed strip of steel; with any luck, it would hold in any crack.

I slipped various implements into various pockets, cursing myself for an idiot all the while.

This shouldn't have been necessary.

One of the most important things to keep nearby is money. I should have thought it all through, but I don't like to have the reputation for carrying a lot on me, and didn't figure to have to, not in the Empire—where my signature normally is quickly redeemable by my shares in the New Pittsburgh project—just as I wouldn't have in Home, where I've let Lou sit on much of my earnings from the raiding years.

In practice, what I usually would have done if I'd needed some coin would be to sign a note with the Imperial Treasurer—well, actually, more likely his clerk, or the castle chamberlain, and let Home and the Empire square accounts later.

But that would have required explanations, and

I didn't want to give out any explanations, or
tempt even somebody as friendly as Jayar to in-
gratiate himself to the Emperor with a quickly
dropped comment. (Or, if I had wanted to give
up being overly cynical for a moment, I could
have just decided that it was better for Jayar that
he didn't know, but you know me; I wouldn't
give up being overly cynical unless the pay was
right . . .)

It's usually much easier to get forgiveness than
to get permission. Particularly when you intend
to be long gone, just in case.

So I slipped a bag over my shoulder, then
slipped my braided leather rope around one of
the brass staples next to the window, slipped into
my climbing gloves, and stepped out into the
dark of night.

There's something to be said for doing what you
do best, no matter what it is, and there was
something special to slipping through the dark of
the night at the base of the residence, nothing
between me and the guards walking their tours
on the walls except air and darkness. Back on the
Other Side, I'd not been clumsy, but I'd never
have been able to slip between the shadows like
a wraith, invisible to all.

And yes, while only an idiot does dangerous
things just for the thrill of it, there was a certain
something to the knowledge that I was once

again taking it all in my own hands. Including, perhaps, getting a little of my own back.

But I'd save the gloating, even private gloating, for later. Emotions could be played out in private later; it was time to exercise talent and skill.

There are no secure buildings, not really—hell, all buildings function as both a container and a shelter. A container is designed primarily to keep something in, and a shelter to keep something out. But what they keep in and what they keep out flows from their design. A jail, for example, is designed to keep a person or persons limited in movement to one space, and most of its design goes toward that end—the locks are on the outside, and the keys kept away; floors, ceilings, and walls are kept smooth so as to make any damage apparent.

It keeps the prisoners from getting out without a whole lot of difficulty.

But getting into a jail isn't usually difficult.

Now, a castle is basically a container designed to keep an army out. The base of the walls slopes out just a touch, so as to allow the residents to drop stones, say, or boiling oil, say, and have both of them splash on anybody trying to get in. Guards walk the parapets with their attention directed outward, and report in regularly so as to alert the authorities by their silence when they've been, well, silenced. (Yes, I've silenced more than a few guards in my time—living out a cliché doesn't bother me—but taking out a guard means you have to be ready to kick everything into high gear. If he lets out a noise when you do it, it's like firing a starting pistol. At best, even if you do it quietly, it's like lighting a fuse of indeterminate length, because everything will hit the fan when he doesn't check in, and you really don't know if you can take him out silently, or how long it'll be until his boss gets suspicious. You'll never find a spherical guard of uniform density when you need one . . . )

The main attention of the defenders is always on the entrances—they're the weak points to invading armies, so they're the parts where extra towers are built, where portcullises sit above traps and moats, and where murder holes look down upon well-designed killing grounds.

But once you get into the inner portion of the castle, the design doesn't tend to restrict movement. Oh, there're a few exceptions. The stairways tend to be narrow, and curve up counterclockwise, to make life easy for a retreating right-handed defender and difficult for a charging right-handed attacker. And certainly the cells in the dungeon aren't designed to allow freedom of movement.

But, largely, the design doesn't make life difficult once you're inside. It's not impossible to design things differently, mind—but that would interfere with the movement of troops inside, which would interfere with the basic function of the structure. It's important to be able to bring your forces to any point to repel a possible invasion—

Even if the design makes life relatively easy for, say, a thief.

It was just a matter of technique: stay in the shadows, where I was all but invisible, until I was sure that there was nobody within view, then move swiftly but silently, weight balanced on the ball of each foot in turn, into the next shadow, and wait, wait, wait, listening.

It took me only a few minutes to make my way around the back of the building and into the shadows at the edge of the main courtyard. The closest call was at the rear entrance to the residence, where I slipped silently into the vines covering the walls while a foursome of guards walked in from their circuit of the walls.

But that wasn't hard, or difficult—I just narrowed my eyes to slits, so no flash of white would give me away, and waited for their footsteps to diminish in the distance. No need to worry about their relief showing up—their relief had found them up on the parapet, or they wouldn't be here.

A lamp flickered high up on the second floor of the main wing, where the Emperor's bedroom suite was located—or, at least, had been back when Karl was the emperor. It had been Prince Pirondael's before Karl, and I didn't have any reason to think that Thomen had changed things, just for the sake of changing things. The way the little bastard was taking to the appurtenances of power, it was a good bet that the room was still his.

The traditional invisible way to do things would have been to rock-climb up the side, digging for finger purchase among the leaves, finding places where the old mortar had given way between the stones, but I was in a hurry, and getting old for this, and more than a little lazy. I took one of a dozen long blackened-steel spikes from my vest, reached above my head and found a soft spot in the earthy mortar, then pushed it in until only six or so inches protruded, then repeated the process, at my waist-level, leaving me somewhere to stand.

I may have been getting old, but I wasn't dead yet, and my abilities hadn't deserted me. In another few seconds, I'd climbed up to the spike and was standing on one foot on it, reaching over my head to repeat the process.

It took me a delightfully short time until I was at the Emperor's mottled-glass window, peeking in.

The window was closed and locked, but the metal shutters hadn't been lowered. No reason, and besides, Thomen hadn't removed the window seat—it would be a nice place to sit and read or write, with fresh air blowing in through the open window and the light of day streaming into the room.

Slipping the lock was no work at all, and then I was inside, the hinges making only the slightest creak.

I stood silently for a long time, listening. There was movement in the hall outside, but nothing here.

It's always good to prepare a back way out—I unlocked the window in the shower room beyond the bedroom, and oiled the hinges with a vial from my bag, making sure they swung open silently.

I let out a sigh that I hadn't realized I'd been holding in, slid the curtains closed, and sat down on the floor until I got my breath back, or at least most of it. I was definitely feeling every minute of my forty-or-so-years as I allowed myself to lean back and stretch out on the thick carpet, for just a moment.

Getting a bit too old for this. A bit too much exertion for one night, although I didn't see a way around this part of it, and wouldn't have missed the previous part for anything.

I took a small candle lantern from my pack, lit it with a long match from a hidden pocket, and then got to work in the flickering, buttery light.

Over on Thomen's desk, a small stack of the

new silver marks, the ones with Thomen's face on
them, held down a sheaf of papers. I took half of
the stack, changed my mind and took all of it,
and then searched through the drawers, taking a
few coins here, a few there. Coins jingle; I
wound each into a soft cloth, then tied the
packet tightly before putting it into my thief's
bag.

A gleaming chamber pot sat next to the table—
Rank Hath Its Privileges—and there was an old
pre-Empire gold candelabra on the table, so I
took the candelabra, figuring that Lack of Rank
Hath Its Privileges, Too.

It only seemed fair, after all, that if Thomen
was going to make it necessary for me to flee
town, he should fund it. I mean, given the situation, my other choices would be to steal from
somebody who didn't deserve it, or to actually
youshouldpardontheexpression work to support
myself as I went hunting for Jason, and that
hardly seemed either convenient or right.

I blew out my candle, tucked it back into my
pack, and slipped back out into the night, closing
the window behind me, slipping the catch back
into place with a small probe.

I thought about leaving the spikes—hidden in
the ivy, they'd hardly draw a lot of attention—but
then decided against it, and drew them out as I
climbed down. Thieving is sort of like camping—

take nothing but pictures, leave nothing but footprints—except different: you want to take a lot more than pictures, and you don't want to leave footprints.

It's also, properly done, a little like magic.

*And now, for my next trick: getting the hell out of here.*

I stood in the darkness to the side of the main entrance and stripped to the skin, wiping my face first with my shirt and then with a damp washcloth from a leather pouch in my bag. I wished for a mirror, but thoroughness would have to serve.

I pulled my clean clothes out of my bag, placing the thief's outfit inside, then slipped the bag's straps over my right shoulder. My casually-flung cloak covered the bag neatly, and, dressed in a gleaming white shirt and shiny leather trousers that nobody would possibly associate with a thief, I walked into the light, and, very publicly, back up to my room. I had a note and an IOU to write, and then it would be time to go.

I blew out the lamp and stood in the dark of the room.

It was all logical, and more than a little reasonable, given the nightmares.

Thomen was going to order me to do something that I didn't want to do, and I had no intention either of conceding or of matching wills with him, not in his Empire, not in his castle.

I didn't have a choice, not with my nightmares turning sweet sleep into a nightly horror show of old men trying to hold back all the demons of hell. It was my subconscious's way of kicking me into doing something important, and that meant getting out on the road, and not just for exercise or some minor errand for the Emperor. I had to do something the back of my mind would recognize as important, or live with the nightmares.

I'll skip the nightmares, thank you very much.

So it was time to get out of Dodge.

We had quartered our horses at a hostler down in the village, so I had access to transportation. I now had money—and a route out of town. A couple of days of hard riding would take me out of the Empire and into Kiar; with a bit of luck, I could pick up Jason's trail on the Cirric coast.

It felt like something was missing, and it took me a moment to realize what it was: I hadn't said goodbye. Not to Aeia, not to Janie and D.A., not to Kirah or Doria. My letter of explanation to Aeia wasn't enough, not emotionally.

Well, screw it. I couldn't delay leaving much longer, or I'd have to drop down into the outer bailey and try to make my way over the outer curtain wall, and while I could do it, the exertions of the evening had already tired me more than they would have ten years before. The last thing I needed before a long night's ride was to wear myself out climbing up and down walls.

So, humming a tune, I threw my rucksack into a large wicker basket, brought the basket up to my shoulder, and walked down the stairs, and out through the open door into the night.

I like the night. Or maybe make that the nights, because there's an infinite variety of them, depending on what you are and what you're doing.

A warm summer night, gentle breezes blowing up a grassy hillock to where I sat with a woman I loved, under a sky so clear, a canopy of stars so bright that I could make out their colors, a slow procession of faerie lights pulsing a heavy blue-to-green adagio off over the horizon—that was different from a coal-black night after a heavy rainstorm, me dressed in black, creeping through darkness barely broken by a shuttered lantern up ahead, watching not only for the guard's back, but for the backup guard, because it surely couldn't be as easy as it seemed—any time it seemed too easy, it was time to reevaluate what was really going on. And both of those were different from a quiet autumn night outside of the Endell warrens, a cold, clammy wind blowing in over the Cirric and the land, waiting for word of a friend's death, the night brightening and warming in my heart if not my skin when I saw a familiar form awkwardly perched on the back of a gelding that would have been gray in the light, as well.

But they all have something in common: you don't see with your eyes, not really—you see with your mind.

As a thief, sneaking around in the darkness, the night had been filled with dark and shadow, too-bright light splashing out carelessly through open doors and undraped windows. Far-off footsteps had thundered like distant drums, while the sound of the wind through the few trees standing within the courtyard was a comforting blanket of white noise into which my own footsteps would disappear.

But now, the night was lit with smoky torches on the battlements, vying with the overhead stars and distant pulsing faerie lights to light up at least a part of the night, and I wasn't sneaking through it: I was marking my place in it, as I headed for the front gate.

During wartime, the gates to the keep had been closed promptly at sunset, and the northern bastion manned as heavily as the barbicans overlooking the main gate. But we were at peace, at least for the time being, and there were barely a dozen soldiers visibly on duty at the gate.

Some things hadn't changed from the old days: high above on the wall, an old soldier stood watch over the main rope, a sharp axe mounted on the wall at a convenient height. The wrought-iron and timbered portcullis could be lowered slowly, as it shortly would be, no doubt, or in case of some urgency it and its twin on the outer gate could be slammed down quickly, perhaps trapping an intruder in the killing ground in between the two, and at least limiting the number of intruders who could make it safely into the outer ward.

Some things had. In the old days, before we had left our imprint on Castle Biemestren, there hadn't been a dark wire running off into the night, and there had been no constant chatter of a telegraph above, as stations up and down the line checked in almost constantly, even when they didn't have any traffic, as a way of announcing that they were still operational, and uninvaded.

I smiled and waved at the guards as I walked out through the gate. Wartime standing orders would have had them stop me, and even in peacetime they certainly had the authority to do that if I left them suspicious, but it was a simple fool-the-mind: you just don't think of somebody making an escape doing it with a bounce in his step and a bulky basket on his shoulder, wearing bright clothes and whistling the coda from *Suite: Judy Blue Eyes*.

Now, if it was the Grateful Dead's _Truckin'_, on the other hand . . .

I had left the keep behind me, and was more than halfway down the dirt road toward the town below, when something stirred in the bushes, and a harsh voice whispered, _"Wait."_

# 6

## The Indeterminate House

When you cannot make up your mind
which of two evenly balanced courses of
action you should take—choose the
bolder.

—W. J. Slim

Boldness is like a condom. If you rely on
it all the time, no matter how good it
is, and no matter how good you are,
eventually it will break.

—Walter Slovotsky

The early-afternoon downpour kept up a madden-
ingly even pace as they paused at the fork in the
Edgerly-Pemburne road, where an ancient stone
carving stood as though waiting for something.

Although, to be honest, Jason could not figure
out what the stone carving was supposed to de-
pict. It could have been a human figure long ago,
although a squat one, arms held close against its
sides. But wind and time had robbed it of all fea-

tures, and all he could tell was that it had once been something.

It was good to think about something other than the rain, and how miserable it made the day. His oiled-canvas poncho had long gone nonwaterproof in spots, and Jason was soaked to the skin. There was nothing to be done about it, except suffer.

The two dwarves kept up a pleasant conversation about metalworking. That had become the default topic for the two of them, and it was driving Jason slowly mad. Or maybe not so slowly, at that.

Nareen shook his head. "All roads lead somewhere," he said. "Put enough steps in a row, and we shall find ourselves at a warm inn."

"East," Ahira decided.

That made sense. The eastern road, so they had been told, swung a bit wider before it looped back toward Pemburne, but it cut through the woods, and that would get them out of the open, and away from the wind that drove the rain in through every seam and dry spot in his poncho.

He stepped up the pace to a fast walk, ignoring the way the dwarves had to hurry to keep up.

"Ease up, eh?" Ahira said. "We'll get there, and we'll be wet when we do."

Nareen the glassmaker didn't say anything. His thin hair was slicked back against his wrinkled scalp, and little rivulets of water worked their way down through his inadequate poncho to run down his bowed legs, but it didn't seem to bother him.

That made sense. Everything the dwarf said made sense, and if there was one thing that Jason Cullinane was more tired of than being scared all the damn time, it was listening to a dwarf making sense.

That was the trouble with traveling with two of the Moderate People, he decided for at least the thousandth time. They always made sense; they spoke gently; they woke up agreeable and went to bed good-humored.

It was driving him fucking crazy. Crazy enough to let his mind wander. Crazy enough to look at alternatives.

The woods arced over the road ahead, promising some relief from the rain, but as they walked down the dark path, gray almost to black under the stormy skies, the promise turned out to be a lie. The leaves dripped cold water just as hard as it rained out in the open, just less rhythmically.

Not an improvement.

"So we put one foot in front of the other, and eventually we'll find ourselves in front of a place that is dry, with a fire to dry our clothes and warm our bones," Ahira said.

"Perhaps sooner than we fear, and certainly later than we would prefer," Nareen said. "Even at my age, one doesn't care to be cold and wet all the time."

"Then why don't you *do* something about it?" Jason asked, fairly sure that most of his irritation was showing through.

"But I am, young one," Nareen said.

"Oh?"

"I am enduring it."

Ahira chuckled.

Jason lowered his head and leaned into the storm.

Edgerly and Pemburne were the usual one day's hard walk apart, but of course that usual measure involved a normal day, when the mud of the road didn't reach up and try to drag down your feet with every step except for those that left you ankle-deep or worse in a puddle, when you didn't try to stay at the edge of the road and brush, walking more on the brush than the road, and when rain and gloom and dark didn't stretch roads out almost interminably.

What Jason wanted was a warm fire to sit by, some warm food to put in his stomach, and a dry place to sleep, preferably with a couple of dogs to keep him warm and comfortable, if a nice fireplace wasn't available.

But it was getting dark, and on a black and rainy night you stayed off the road in the dark. Too many ways to go wrong, when you couldn't see where you were stepping, and anything that produced enough light would make you an easy target for anybody lying in wait. There was no need to be paranoid about it, to assume that this next bend in the road was where somebody hostile waited, but it was time to get off the road and bed down for the night. The elf-light from a glowsteel in his pack meant they didn't have to either panic or impose on Nareen's magic to light their way as they made camp, but it was going to be another night out in the rain.

What he'd have to settle for, again, would be a night in the woods just off the main trail, some cold jerky and dried corn from his pack, and at best a flickering fire that would hiss and sputter all night, barely enough to warm him and not nearly enough to dry him off as he slouched against the bole of a tree, halfway between interminable, red-eyed awakeness and only the lightest of sleeps. He would be woken up in the gray of predawn by some sound, and after making sure that his fire was out, as though the weather wouldn't take care of that for him, he and the two Moderate People would slosh off into the day.

It wasn't the dangers of the road that bothered him, not as much as the constant oppression of it.

Up ahead, at the top of the next hill, a building stood waiting as the rain poured down and the sky went from dark gray to darker.

For a moment, it looked familiar to Jason. It reminded him, of all things, of the sort of entry-
buildings that the Andirdell dwarves built outside
their warrens—it was a low, one-storied building,
curved as though it had been built up against
something, although there was nothing there for
it to have been built up against.

Or maybe there was. He couldn't see anything
much beyond it, except for darkness.

Hard to tell.

Nareen smiled. "I think we shall sleep warm
and well, young Cullinane," he said. "With our
bellies filled with a thick soup of"—he paused to
sniff at the air—"carrots and mushrooms and barley and just a trace of turnip and onion, and oily,
oily garlic. Perhaps with our heads buzzing with
rich brown beer, or even some old wine."

"If you knew that there was an inn up
ahead . . ."

The old dwarf smiled. "Well, I told you there
was. It was just a question of how far up ahead.
And which inn. Until you see it for yourself, the
answers to most questions are indeterminate."

Somehow, the mud seemed to weigh Jason's
feet down even more, while his legs had somehow become lighter. The prospect of spending a
night warm and dry almost pushed him to a run,
as badly as he didn't want to appear impatient
and immature in front of Ahira and the other
dwarf.

Besides, he didn't know who would be there. He gave a hitch to his swordbelt and a pat to the hidden brace of pistols under his soaked poncho. The odds of either pistol firing were negligible, given the time they and he had spent out in the rain. That was the nice thing about a sword: it was always loaded, it worked wet or dry, and it never misfired.

Ahira had hitched at his battleaxe, too, then glanced at Jason with a too-flat expression that might as well have said that he wished to have somebody else at his side.

Which was exactly backwards, Jason decided. Chasing after Mikyn was Jason's job, and nobody else's. The question was not whether or not Jason was good enough to back up Ahira, but whether or not Ahira was an appropriate companion to Jason.

Ahira must have caught him smiling. "What are you thinking?"

"Whether or not you're the right person to be covering my back at the moment," Jason said.

Ahira laughed. "You Cullinanes always have had a strange sense of humor."

It looked for all the world like an Andirdell-style warren entrance: curved, fitted stones carved to look more like the side of a gray mountain than a building; the door a low half-circle of oak, its hinges hidden, a huge iron doughnut hanging from a thick chain in its center.

Nareen was reaching for it when the door swung open, wafting delicious odors of food and warmth from the brightness beyond.

"Master Nareen and friends, be welcome," a deep voice thrummed in Dwarvish. "Enter my home in peace, and stay in peace." The accent was one Jason couldn't place—the vowels were stretched, the consonants clipped. Sort of like a combination of Endell and Andirdell accents, but with a Pandathaway Erendra overlay.

Jason stooped to follow the dwarves inside, to the mudroom, where a particularly large dwarf, a head taller and a fist's-breadth wider than Ahira, stood with a raised brass lantern clasped in his hamlike fist. Beneath a massive, ugly nose and a coal-black beard that covered his thick chin and neck like curly moss, his smile was broad and white.

"How good to see you again, Master Nareen."

"And you as well, good Sulluren. How is your wife?"

"Busy in the kitchen, I can assure you!" the dwarf said. "There will be rolls fresh from the oven, baked to the lightest brown, and served with ramekins of yellowy butter, and vats of my own mushroom and barley soup, and a mushroom casserole of my own recent creation—the secret is to slice the caps ever so thinly, and then cook them for the veriest instant in rendered duckfat, and then to—"

"And then, perhaps, to invite us in?" Nareen asked. "Where perhaps there's a warm seat by a fire to warm our bones and dry our clothes?"

Jason was completely confused. If Nareen knew the dwarf innkeeper, then he ought to know where they were, but either he had lied or . . .

"My manners, but of course." Sulluren set his lantern down so violently that Jason wondered for a moment if it might either go out or smash something inside and douse them all with flaming oil, but no, all it did was *thuck* its base into the mud.

Thick hands helped with packs and ponchos, as Sulluren relieved all three of them of their burdens, handling their gear with surprising ease.

The dwarf dug the big toe of one of his sandaled feet into the mud beneath the edge of the lantern, and even though he couldn't possibly have seen the carrying handle, flipped it up into the air and caught it neatly on one extended finger.

He smiled up at Jason. "A few centuries of doing something constantly, young Cullinane, and one gets fairly good at it. Even if that something is as modest an occupation as one of innkeeper. But please, come with me."

There was a right angle turn just beyond the mudroom into a low passageway, its stone floor lined with mud scrapers along one side, and opposite a wall filled with carved crannies, now mostly empty.

"There is only one more guest in residence this night," Sulluren said. "I suspect my rates prove too stiff for the casual traveler."

Jason didn't like the sound of that, but Ahira just patted his arm. "I take it you'll take a gold draft on King Maherallen?" he asked.

"Of course," Sulluren said. "He still owes you rather a lot, although I doubt he's happy about your long absence—still, a debt is a debt."

Jason leaned his head next to Ahira. "You know this dwarf, this place?"

Ahira shrugged. "Yes and no. I'd thought that Sulluren's Indeterminate Inn had gone legendary."

Sulluren laughed. "As well you should have, friend Ahira. I go to some trouble to keep it so. I'd hardly care to be overwhelmed with guests if it was known that the Inn was still sometimes to be found in the Eren regions. In fact, I doubt that you would have found me at all, if Vair the Uncertain hadn't lent a hand."

"Vair?"

"Who better to help arrange a rendezvous between unlikely allies at a place of no fixed location?"

"Unlikely allies?"

"Patience, young Cullinane, patience is an expression of the virtue of moderation."

Another right turn brought them into a wide, low room, dark, lit only by the huge, man-high fireplace at the far end, and light streaming out through slatted blinds to the left.

"Your boots, if you please," Sulluren said, gesturing toward a low bench. Following the dwarves' example, Jason sat, and pulled off his wet boots, accepting Sulluren's offer of a soft towel to clean and dry his cold, wet wrinkled feet; he had rarely felt anything as pleasant as the feel of the thick, warm towel between his toes.

"Warm robes will be along shortly; they are being heated on stones at the moment," Sulluren said, bustling off with the boots. "In the meantime, I would suggest you make yourselves comfortable by the fire." He walked through the slatted door.

Jason padded across the thickest, softest rug he had ever felt, toward the fire, past a thick, low table.

Nareen's smile was even broader than usual as he squatted near the fire. "It's been a long time since I've been here," he said, rubbing his knob-knuckled fingers together disturbingly close to the flame.

"Do you mind telling me about it?" Jason asked, more than a little irritated at the way his companions were taking all this strangeness for granted.

"Little to tell, little that I know. The location of

the Indeterminate Inn is, well, largely indeterminate. I've heard it claimed that it's built into the structure of reality itself; those who would know say little. I can tell you that we'll see no staff save for Sulluren, our host, that his fees will be large relative to our present finances, but still affordable, and that there's somebody—somebody who does no magic—waiting to meet us here, somebody sent by Vair the Uncertain."

Ahira snorted. "And how would you know all that?"

"Well, I know that the location of the Indeterminate Inn is indeterminate not merely because of what I've heard but because I've been here before, and it wasn't here, if you understand what I mean. And I know we'll see nothing of his wife and servants because although Sulluren claims to have a wife and servants, nobody's ever seen any staff here save Sulluren, and those few who announced an intention to try too hard to find such have either reported themselves frustrated or never been seen again. And I know that this night will be expensive because all who have stayed in the Inn have reported that they could afford, if just barely, Sulluren's fees.

"And I know that we'll meet somebody sent here by Vair the Uncertain because while I don't see the flames of a wizard, I feel the presence of a human holding an amulet whose crystal I once made for Vair the Uncertain," the dwarf said, turning. "He lurks right there." A thick hand gestured toward a dark archway.

"Quite so." A shape moved out of the far corridor and into the firelight: a medium-tall man, moving easily across the carpet, his face lit by the gentle green glow of the gem that dangled from a silver chain looped elegantly around the fingers of his right hand.

He moved into the light, his hands held out, palms first. The white sleeves of his shirt and the darker ones of his overshirt had been rolled up almost to the elbow; there was nothing strapped to them, and his palms were well away from the wire-wound hilt of the sword at his waist.

He was perhaps a year or two older than Jason, but built slimly, almost effeminately so, slim not quite to the point of skinniness, his close-cropped beard carefully sculpted to maximize the pointiness of his chin.

"Good evening," he said, his voice too smooth. "I am Toryn, at your service."

Jason's hand was resting on the hilt of his sword. "Jason, Baron Cullinane, greets you," he said, formally.

A smile played across the other's lips. "Ah. You will have it formal? Very well: Toryn, Journeyman Slaver, greets you."

A slaver? Ahira's thick fingers were on the wrist of Jason's sword hand. "You are here under an oath of truce?" the dwarf asked.

"Sworn to and bound by Vair the Uncertain," Toryn said. "It was he and the Guildmaster who sent me in this direction." His smile revealed too-white teeth. "He said it wasn't utterly impossible that I might find you out this way."

That sounded like Vair.

Ahira looked up at Jason. "You ask him the next question," he said, suddenly the teacher.

"What did you swear to and how do we know you mean it?"

"A good question. An obvious one, perhaps, but a good one." Moving only his right hand, Toryn raised the amulet to his forehead. His form seemed to waver in the flickering firelight, and then to stretch and lengthen, his thickly curled and heavily oiled ringlets of hair lightening and straightening while his beard thinned and shortened until it was gone, leaving behind only smooth skin over the sharp, pointed jaw.

The image wavered until it was Vair the Uncertain who seemed to stand before him, and it was the elf's voice that was pitched as a tenor but somehow had a feel of baritone in it that answered, "And, with your will, Toryn, I bind you to neither threaten nor permit damage to Jason Cullinane or his companions, this binding to last until your return to the city of Pandathaway or until you are attacked by Jason Cullinane or any of his companions. I give you my voice and my image to repeat my words, but only so long as you hold my amulet and are bound by this geas."

The hand dropped, and Toryn's form melted back into his own. "We have a problem in common," he said. "Guildmaster Yryn has sent me hunting you, hoping that I might be of aid." He raised a hand to his forehead. "As I said, I am at your service." He gestured to a table. "Will you sit? We have, I would suspect, much to discuss."

Jason didn't like his smile.

Jason, his arms folded across his chest, sat back as Toryn nibbled at a chicken leg crusted over with sage and garlic. He hadn't intended to break bread with the slaver, but hunger had changed his mind. When the platter of chicken had arrived at the table, the smell had been absolutely maddening. The food still smelled wonderful, even with his stomach full and his brain ever so slightly humming from the wine he'd downed.

Ahira had long since finished eating, as had Nareen. The dwarf wizard sat back in his chair, his sausagelike fingers folded comfortably about his middle, his eyes closed as though asleep, although Jason didn't believe for a moment that Nareen really was asleep.

"It's really rather simple," Toryn said from around a mouthful. "There's a commonality of interest between the Guild and the Cullinanes, at least for the moment. You have the equivalent of a rogue brother out there, and we have a definite nuisance to deal with. There are two schools of thought in Pandathaway—one is that it is your father, and the other is that it is another one of your accursed raiders being," he considered the next word for a moment, "naughty." He raised a slim eyebrow. "Unless you have changed your longstanding policy against property owners?"

"Slave owners," Jason said. Ahira's body language and his whispers told him not to pick a fight, but this was a slaver sitting opposite from him. Everything he had ever learned said to go for his weapons and make the slaver dead.

Toryn dismissed it with an airy wave. "I don't propose to debate matters of right and wrong with you. I do propose to aid you in a matter of our mutual benefit," he said, touching a finger to his hairline in sketchy salute, "subject to your orders, and, of course, my geas."

"And find out whether or not this Warrior really is my father," Jason said. "Since none of you was ever able to stop him . . ."

"I never claimed to be acting other than in our interest." Toryn took another nibble. "But if it was only that knowledge I was after, I would simply trick it out of you rather than join you—and please do note that I am joining you at some risk to my person. Now, have we an arrangement?"

"What's in it for us?"

"Horses, for one. And more." Toryn tapped at a

breast pocket. "Our Guildmaster has bought some spells from some of the better wizards in Pandathaway. I can't tell you where your Warrior will strike next, but I can tell you where he likely will strike soon." He smoothed his tunic over the pocket. "I ask you one last time: have we an arrangement, Jason Cullinane?"

The obvious question was whether, if the Guild knew that, they had already dispatched a dozen or more assassins to lie in wait, and the only answer to that was, of course.

This was, for them, just another bit of insurance. Assuming that Toryn was telling the truth. The Guild had, one way or other, come up on the losing side every time they had fought the Cullinanes, and it made sense from their point of view to work out a deal.

The only trouble was, it also made sense from Jason's point of view. Toryn knew something that Jason needed to know, and Jason was by no means certain that the information was in the pocket that Toryn was advertising.

Ahira looked over at him. "Nareen," he said, his eyes on Jason, not on the older dwarf, "can you tell if he's speaking the truth?"

Nareen opened an eye. "Of course." He produced a small red lens and brought it up to his eye, considering the slaver for a moment. "On the geas, of course; as to the rest, it . . . appears to be truthful." The dwarf wizard tucked the lens back in his pouch, refolded his hands across his middle, and again closed his eyes. "It hardly would appear to be complete."

Toryn's smile widened. "Would you expect me to tell you everything I know?"

Ahira shrugged. "It's up to you, Jason. Call it."

It was ridiculous. The right thing to do with a slaver was to kill it dead, to leave the body where its friends would find it, or mount its head on a pole. Let the rest of them know who did it; let the rest of them sleep lightly, wake constantly during the night, fearing the soft sound of a sword cleaving the air toward them.

Karl Cullinane would have known how to deal with a slaver, and that wouldn't include negotiations.

But if Jason didn't come to terms here and now with this slaver, he might never find Mikyn. He had thought of traveling into Pandathaway, to try at some great risk to trick whatever information the Guild had out of them, and here it was being offered to him, as on a platter. All he had to do was say yes.

He was opening his mouth to say no when Toryn rose. "You might wish to discuss it among yourselves," the slaver said, turning and walking closer to the hearth, idly picking up a poker and poking at the glowing coals.

Ahira leaned his head closer. "Tell me."

"My mind says to say yes, but my gut says to

leap over the table and grab the slaver by his throat."

Nareen's eyes didn't open. "Not a wise idea, all things considered. Sulluren is famous for not allowing his guests to hurt one another."

"Right. Don't . . . abuse the hospitality," Ahira said. "Still, I'm sure this Toryn knows something—do you think we should try to track him, see if he'll lead us to Mikyn?"

Jason shook his head. "You know better. If we don't deal with him, that would be our obvious move. It would be too easy for him to set up an ambush—"

"There's that geas. He can't."

Jason snorted. "And you know for a fact that there's not another slaver waiting over the next hill, carrying a potion or charm to dispel the geas?"

It made his stomach churn, but it was the right move. His father couldn't have done it.

*But I'm not my father,* Jason thought. *And maybe Karl Cullinane wouldn't have been able to find Mikyn.*

*To hell with it.*

He stood, his mouth tasting of fear and ashes. "Toryn," Jason said, "we have a deal."

Smiling in an infuriatingly superior sort of way, Toryn resumed his seat, apparently ignoring Jason's glare, then called to Sulluren for more wine.

"Then let us first swear to it on our blades, and then drink to it, and then rest ourselves well, for tomorrow we take horse away from here."

"Where?"

"We start in Pemburne, and then to Dunden and Murdalk's End."

Jason cocked his head to one side. "We were already on the road to Pemburne—"

"As was I," Toryn said, with that same smile. "It was not impossible that I might run into your Warrior before you did, and save all the . . ." he waved a hand at Jason and Ahira ". . . bother." He raised his glass. "To our partnership."

Jason raised his own glass. "To success." He hoped the wine would wash the bad taste out of his mouth, but it didn't. He drained the glass and poured himself another one.

Jason wasn't used to drinking quite so much; Jason wasn't much used to drinking; it got a bit blurry after that. He remembered bits and pieces of it later—Ahira telling him the long version of how Tennetty lost her eye, and Toryn's dark complexion whitening a full shade; he remembered Sulluren joining them for a small bottle of dessert wine so dark purple it was almost black, and so sweet and rich and fruity that it seemed to cling to his tongue for days; and Nareen the Glassmaker, his wrinkled forehead sweaty from the

drink and the blaze of the fireplace, his voice a
sweet, rich baritone, breaking into a dwarvish
ballad that had been old when Nareen was
young; and he remembered Toryn as a poor storyteller and better listener.

But that was all in bits and pieces.

Mostly he remembered saying goodbye to
Nareen: the dwarvish handshake, with the glass-
making wizard's bony hand clasping Jason's fore-
arm while he clasped the ropy muscles in
Nareen's, and Nareen's sad comments that he
had done all he could, but that their paths must
now separate.

He didn't remember many of the words, except
for: "You must be who you are, young Cullinane;
the son is not the shadow of the father, though
truth to tell, the taller the father, the harder it
will be to escape the shadow."

"I don' unnerstan'," he said, cursing himself silently for the slurring of his words, and again for
repeating himself. "I'm sorry, N'reen, but I don'
unnerstan'."

He remembered Nareen's smile. It was good to
remember a friend's smile.


He woke in the gray morning to the peppery,
garlicy, meaty smells of sausage cooking, and
found himself under his blankets on the hard
ground, and Ahira crouched over the morning

cookfire, while Toryn tended a trio of grazing horses over across the road.

Nareen, Sulluren, and the Indeterminate Inn were gone.

# 7

## In Which I Find Some Companionship on and for the Road

Waiting around isn't an annoyance; in the right hands, it's an art form.
—WALTER SLOVOTSKY

I always have a fallback position, whenever I take a risk: if all else fails, I'll die horribly, at great length, in great pain. Mind you, it's not a *good* fallback position . . .
—WALTER SLOVOTSKY

For me, I guess it all started one summer at Lake Bemidji. Neat place—a lake large enough to be interesting, but not like one of the Great Lakes or the Cirric; you didn't have to be afraid of it, usually. We rented a cabin there one summer; I was maybe five, my brother Steve a couple of years older.

I don't remember much about it, except fragments: the statues of Paul Bunyan and Babe the

Blue Ox by the shore; the way that the water on the dock outside our cabin seemed absolutely full of tiny sunfish, so eager to be hooked that you could snag them with a fistful of line, a hook, and a few pieces of raw bacon.

And the day it hailed.

Emma—Mom—was never much for fish, be it catching, cleaning, or eating, but Big Mike and Stash had gotten tired of catching sunfish from the dock, so they rented a little boat, about the size of a rowboat, and took it and my brother Steve and me out into the middle of the lake.

We rode out on a little boat with a little motor until we were far, far away from shore, and started fishing. Stash got himself a pickerel, I think, and I know Big Mike got his first muskie because we heard about it for years, and Steve and I each had landed some decent-sized perch.

We were having such a good time catching fish that we didn't notice that it was getting dark, and not because it was late, but because a storm was coming up out of the west.

It started raining, and Stash—he was still Daddy to me— and Big Mike took a look at each other and Big Mike tilted back his Mets cap and gave a shrug that said, *If it was you and me, I'd say to hell with it, let's get wet, but we got the kids with us,* and Daddy nodded once, just once.

So Big Mike started the tiny little outboard motor and we headed back to shore.

It was about then that the hail started. The first one hit near the boat with a loud plop that carried even over the hissing of the rain. And then there was another and another and then they started hitting the boat.

Not just tiny little hailstones either, but big ones, some the size of big marbles. It was like being in a rock fight with God.

Well, Stash took his shirt off and wrapped it around me, and Big Mike took his cap off and put it on Steve, and the two of them told us to lie down in the bottom of the boat, and while hail drummed down out of the sky, Dad and Big Mike huddled over us, sometimes grunting when a bigger hailstone hit them.

Big Mike ran the boat right up on shore, and he grabbed Steve while Stash grabbed me, and the two of them ran up to the covered porch of the cabin, where the hail still slammed down, like a box of marbles emptied onto a wooden board.

Emma had the light on. I still remember how bright it seemed, even during the day, and how strange it seemed to me that she'd have it on in the afternoon like that.

God, they were battered. Stash had sort of folded his hands over his head, but when Mom gently stripped off his shirt, his back was bruised in dozens of places, already purpling in spots; and Big Mike's bald head was cut open, blood run-

ning down the side of his face, mixing with the
water.

And Mom was just this side of hysterical, not
that I blamed her.

Stash ended up comforting *her.* "Everything's
just fine, Emma," he said, taking her face gently
in his hands and making her look at Steve and
me.

"Everything's okay, Em," Big Mike said, smiling
like he'd won a prize.

Funny thing is, with Stash bruised and Big
Mike bloody, they both meant it. What they
meant was *the kids are okay.*

The situation called for lightning reflexes, either
to come up with a snappy response to the hissed
whisper or to whip out an edged or blunt object.

"Huh?" I said.

Bren Adahan stepped out onto the road, a
smile on his face that I would have been happy to
have the occasion to wipe off—say, with some
coarse sand and a brick.

"I thought we had an agreement," he said.

I'd seen that expression before, although it had
been many years, and not on his face. It had been
on a big screen, and the line had been, "I'm
shocked, Rick, shocked that there's gambling going on here."

His evening finery had been exchanged for
dark jacket and trousers and heavy boots, suitable

for the road, and a well-used rucksack was on his back. "Something about our working together, the next time you went out on the road?"

All too damn clever. Somebody had worked out what I was up to, and I didn't think that Bren was up to following the machinations of my mind. If he was, I had seriously underestimated him, and that was bad.

I shrugged. "Sure: we agreed that when I took Andy out for a little jaunt, you'd come along and keep us company. I don't see her here."

He *tsk*ed as he shook his head. "I wouldn't have thought you'd violate even the spirit of our agreement, Walter Slovotsky." He took a few steps down the road, then turned and waited. "Well, I can hardly come along with you if you don't come along with me, eh?"

"If you know so much, where are we headed?"

He snorted. "Well, I guess we could be headed toward the cobbler—but I'd rather go to the stables."

Well, somebody had to be the straight man. "Eh? The cobbler?"

"Me, I'd rather wear out a horse than my shoes, but it's your call, Walter. You're in charge."

I won't say I'm equipped to enjoy the inevitable, but I am equipped to recognize it. "Let's go.—Just one thing?"

"Aeia," he said.

"Eh?"

His smile was just one inch shy of overt insult. "Aeia told me that you'd be leaving tonight, and I've got to congratulate her for that when we get back, even if she did overreach."

Well, she had promised to trust me, but she hadn't promised not to think about what I'd do and act appropriately. Which suggested that she thought that Adahan really would be of use on the road.

But did I trust her judgment? It was my neck, not hers, and I've always liked making my own decisions where my neck is concerned.

Bren Adahan hefted a bag that clinked. "I come with funds; I just had the chamberlain cash a draft."

Idiot. And so much for Aeia's judgment. The last thing I needed was for the baron to announce that some of us were leaving—"And what did you tell him?"

He shrugged. "Just that I was going to be buying some breeding stock while I was in the capital, and that we all know that Biemish stallions are the most valued and fecund in the Middle Lands—he suggested I double the draft." Adahan chuckled. "You wouldn't believe what Aeia said you'd do to finance the trip."

I made a private deal with myself: one more time, and if he demanded a straight line after that, I'd get to kill him. "In what way?"

"Oh, she said something about how you'd have pilfered some valuables from the castle."

I'm not sure whether I felt clever or stupid when I pulled the gold candelabra out of my bag and tossed it to him.

His mouth opened, then closed. "We'd better get going," he said.

"Well, yeah," I said. I held out the mouth of my bag for the candelabra. "Trick or treat," I said.

"Eh?"

"Sorry." I switched back to Erendra. "That was English for 'give me the candelabra right this moment.' "

"Compact language, this English of yours. I should learn more sometime."

Reclaiming our four horses—we took Aeia's and Andy's, as well as our own—was easy, and so was the decision to take the southern fork road away from Biemestren, toward Kiar, at least for the first few miles.

Telegraph wire was strung all along the northern road, and it soon would—or at least could—be chattering with instructions to arrest me for various offenses, real and imagined.

The road was a long, twisting gray band in the starlight, laid out along the crest of the gently rolling hills, punctuated every now and then by a sharp twist or intersecting road. The nearest of the Prince's Inns was a full day's ride away from the capital, of course, but by switching mounts we could probably make it well before morning, grab a quick meal and head on out, skipping one night's sleep, just in case there was somebody on our trail.

Just a matter of staying a few steps ahead of the law.

Eventually, of course, Thomen would think better of it. No matter how irritated he was with me, in the long run he wasn't going to either risk a real breach with Home by pushing it too hard or publish the story of how after being imperiously (or imperially) summoned to the Presence, I'd absconded with the silverware. The first would be politically dangerous; the second would make him a laughingstock.

I chuckled to myself. For once, I was grateful to his mother. Hating me though she did, she was devoted to her son, and would keep his welfare in mind, and starting up with the likes of, well, me didn't fit with looking out for him. I mean, I may not have earned it, but I do have a reputation.

Ahead, the road forked off, one fork toward Kiar, another back toward Barony Cullinane.

Adahan was a bit slow; when I took the fork back toward the barony, it took him a full second before he shouted, "Hey! Wait!" and another minute to kick his horse into a canter, leading the two spare horses behind him.

I hadn't thought he'd work it out. Just as well.

He caught up with me.

"Well?"

"Well, what?"

"Well, Walter Slovotsky, this is the road to Barony Cullinane, not toward Kiar."

I would have said that he had a keen eye for the obvious, but I've said that too much and try to repeat myself only when it amuses somebody.

Then again, I'm somebody. "You, Baron, have a keen eye for the obvious."

He didn't like that.

"I thought about it," I said. "You try. We can either ride off in the general direction we think Ahira and Jason are going, and spend more time in the saddle than I care to think about before we cross what's likely to be a cold trail—meanwhile, by the way, ducking whoever it is that Thomen has out looking for us, because you just know that if he sends anybody after us, it's going to be along the road out of the Empire. Or—"

"Or?"

"Or we can head back to the barony, where in about five days, Ellegon's due on his regular route. We can stop by Home, pick up a team of trackers, and when we cross either Mikyn's or Jason's trail, spread out, with Ellegon running interference and communication. Which makes more sense to you?"

His headshake was both rueful and admiring.

"Let's ride," I said. I spurred the horse into a

canter before he worked out that this option meant he was going to spend the nights with Kirah and his smile turned self-satisfied enough to make me want to punch it away.

The wind brought the sound of hoofbeats of two horses at a fast canter from behind us—far behind us, but none too near—in the dark; I spurred my horse into a faster canter. I was leading Aiea's ruddy brown mare, and it protested for a moment, holding back until I gave the hackamore a good pull. I mean, if my horse could canter with me on its back, the least the brown one could do was keep up.

Adahan kept up with me easily; the mottled gelding he was leading trotted along so obediently I suspected he had gone ahead and done what I should have done with my spare horse: put a bit in his mouth and led it by the reins to make it, a er, bit more cooperative.

Problem: what the hell to do? That depended, of course, on what they intended to do about us. Had they been sent off to catch us on our way to Castle Cullinane? Or were they messengers with instructions for Doria to have us arrested? Or . . .

Think of a recon patrol as a guard: you never want to jump them until you're sure you can deal with the consequences.

Ahead, the road forked again: the left would take us toward Barony Cullinane, the right toward Tyrnael. When in doubt, give them the wrong answer: I kicked my horse into a fast canter for a few hundred yards, and led Bren down the road toward Tyrnael, before letting the animal drop down into a trot, and then a walk.

Adahan was shaking his head as he caught up with me. The hoofbeats behind us were quieter, more distant than before, but all that meant was that we had put some distance between us and them.

A wheatfield, the grain chest high, spread out on our right. In the daytime it would have been all warm and golden, but it was night, and under the flickering stars and pulsing faerie lights it looked all white and gray and spooky. To the left, a wedge of woods rose to block out the night sky. A fine place for hiding.

Adahan smiled, then whispered, "Follow me," and spurred his horse into the field, tromping down the grain for at least twenty, thirty yards while I just sat there for a moment.

Idiot. The beaten-down wheat would mark his passing for anybody who bothered to look, even if he made it to and over the slight rise before our pursuers rode by. He likely would, but it wouldn't do us any good.

On the other hand, neither would me ducking into the woods by myself, forgetting for a moment that trying to ride through wooded land in the dark is a terrific way to get scratched at least, get clotheslined by some dark branch quite probably, and/or lose an eye. So, cursing the highborn idiot under my breath, I tugged hard on the rope of the horse I was leading, and kicked my horse after him.

By the time the two horsemen rode by, we were over the rise, our horses hitched to a marker post in the depression beyond, and back just at the rise, the tops of the wheat tickling my nose and ears. Any idiot pursuing us would have seen the path through the grass, but the horsemen, both of them in what appeared even from this distance to be black and silver Imperial livery, barely even gave it a glance.

And then they were gone, and we were left in the dark, the breeze cool, the night insects chittering in their mild amusement.

Ooops. If they'd been looking for us—for anyone—they would have noticed the path. The fact that they didn't meant that they weren't, that it was just a couple of couriers being sent to Barony Tyrnael, not anybody in hot pursuit, that my original notion that I could be long gone before Thomen could decide to send somebody after me still made sense, and that I'd just, well, if not panicked, overreacted.

I could have jumped up and down and shouted to the skies, _I never, ever overreact_, and then stabbed my horse in frustration, but I don't think that would have made the point.

Switching horses made more sense, so we did.

"Not everybody is after you, Walter Slovotsky," Adahan said, as he loosened the rear cinch of his saddle and moved it to his spare horse. "Even if you do try to make things happen that way."

"One point for you, Baron."

He snickered. "One question?"

"Yes?"

"Can we get going now, or do you just want to stand there?"

That wasn't a question I wanted to answer with words; I just set the bit squarely in the mouth of the horse I was going to lead—who says I can't learn—tightened the cinch around the belly of Aeia's stocky horse, and then swung to its back and kicked it into a fast walk.

Night riding goes well with wondering. I wondered when Bren would ask why, if I was going to Castle Cullinane from the first, I'd needed to supply myself with money by ripping off Thomen.

And I wondered what I'd answer, if I'd say that Thomen had needed a lesson about not screwing around with us, and that it had been both my duty and my pleasure to administer it; I wondered if I'd say that if I hadn't ripped him off, he might have wondered what I was going to do for ·money and could well have sent somebody to

Castle Cullinane to find out if that destination was the answer.

I wondered if I'd tell him the truth: that it hadn't occurred to me until we were safely on the road and an idle thought had reminded me that the dragon was due in, and that a side trip to the barony would save weeks of traveling, and bring Ellegon in on everything.

But he never did ask, and we made the trip to Castle Cullinane in record time.

I was stretched out on a cot in the courtyard behind the Castle Cullinane residence tower, the early morning sun warming me, while a bedewed glass of chilled herb tea sat on the stones near my elbow. I'd had the pleasure of the company of Doria and my daughters for breakfast, and the somewhat mixed pleasure of Bren Adahan and Kirah having slept in, or at least having kept to their rooms for the morning, which kept the room temperature comfortable.

The girls had gone off on their various plans for the day—having Daddy around was no big treat for them, not after the first day—and Doria had some things to oversee at the farm, and I was practicing the art of waiting patiently, an art that is best practiced horizontal, with refreshments nearby.

Off in the distance, leathery wings beat the air, triggering a chorus of shouts over by the barracks.

If I'd opened my eyes, I would have seen people waving to Ellegon as he banked in for a landing.

I heard a familiar roar, felt the ground shudder to a familiar *thunk*, and then a familiar voice in my head.

*Good morning, Walter.*

I opened my eyes and rolled to my feet to see Ellegon settling down onto the stones of the courtyard, while a team of burly men from the house guard set up the ladder against his broad side, emptying his load of packages.

Ellegon: a bus-length of gray-green dragon, huge vaguely saurian head eyeing me with an expression that would have looked disapproving even if he hadn't meant it, which he probably did. Truth to tell, I would have left him chained in that Pandathaway sewer; Karl letting him loose almost got the lot of us killed, and I wouldn't want to deprive the universe of Stash and Emma's baby boy.

"Anything interesting?" I asked.

*A couple of letters for Doria, a new saddle for Andrea and a doll for Doranne. Various and sundry.*

"No emergencies pending?"

He snorted. *I predict interesting times. There are emergencies pending all over the Eren regions—in case you hadn't noticed, there's been an epidemic of strange things coming out of Faerie.*

I let that pass. Not only had I noticed, but I'd

The Road Home   163

been at least peripherally useful in stopping the flow, as the dragon knew damn well.

"You mind running a couple of errands with me?"

*I guess that would depend on what they are.*

"Well, for one thing, I'm about to become awfully unpopular around here—"

*Who is she?*

Well, there were some honest answers to that—like Andrea, in one sense. She wasn't going to be thrilled with me ducking out instead of bringing her along. But not for this; this could get sticky, and no matter how impressive she was in the gym, the real world's much messier.

Aeia, of course, in another sense.

But there was no need to go into that now. *Shh,* I thought at the dragon. *Nothing like that.— and for another, I think Jason and Ahira might be able to use a hand.* Never mind that I needed to chase the nightmares away; put it in terms that the dragon would likely understand and accept.

*Then again, maybe I can understand nightmares, and just possibly you should not be quite so condescending.*

*Hey, it's my head. What I think to myself between my very own ears is something you should have the decency to pretend you don't hear.*

Flame roared. *True enough.*

*So?*

*So what?*

*So, are you in on this?*

\*Well, the next stop on my route is supposed to be Biemestren.\*

That was easy to handle; he could unload his cargo for Biemestren here—

\*—I could do any number of things. The question is whether or not I should.\*

*You like being the mailman?*

\*Well, yes, I do. We each contribute in our own way, and with everybody and his brother cultivating dragonbane these days, I'd just as soon stay out of unfriendly territory, lest before asking 'Are you a good witch or a bad witch,' somebody sends another dragonbaned bolt into my otherwise none-too-tender hide.\*

*Fair enough.* He had a point. What with the various things that had been leaking out of Faerie, and the fact that dragonbane was a poison not only to dragons but to most magical metabolisms, the cultivation of dragonbane was becoming awfully common, after many years—there just hadn't been any use for the stuff until recently. But now, all over the Eren regions, people had dragonbaned bolts and arrows ready to fly. It made sense for Ellegon to give this one a bye.

\*True enough. But if I was sensible, I wouldn't be doing this. I take it you're ready to leave?\*

I didn't bother to open my eyes as I smiled. "Better call Adahan, and let's go." Maybe the dragon could pull him out of bed with Kirah.

Ellegon just looked at me, and had the grace to say nothing about the hypocrisy inherent in that thought.

*Where?* is all he asked.

"First Home, and then Pandathaway."

*Let's fly.*

# 8

## Pemburne

*Honi soit qui mal y pense.*
　　—MOTTO OF THE ORDER OF THE GARTER

Relax; the universe *is* out to get you.
　　　　　　　　　　　　—WALTER SLOVOTSKY

Baking in the late afternoon sun, the ramshackle guardhouse outside the low wall surrounding the township of Pemburne was manned by a short troop of horsemen, accompanied by a dozen young boys holding spare mounts, and Jason didn't like that much at all. A confrontation between armed men could only end with a negotiation, fight, flight, or some combination, and while a township whose lord tended to go for a fight all too often would itself be a proper and likely victim of surrounding towns, their lords insisting on mercantile peace if nothing else, Jason didn't like to count on the enlightened self-interest of township lords and lordlings.

Flight didn't seem likely, not with the locals having fresh horses and Jason, Ahira, and Toryn weary on the backs of their tired mounts.

Neither did he like the chances of the three of them taking on a dozen well-armed and well-armored soldiers, two armed with slaver rifles, several with short bows, and all with swords.

Jason stopped counting the worn pommels of the swords at six in a row. Veterans, all of them.

Toryn raised an open palm. "Toryn, Journeyman of the Slavers Guild, greets you, and asks that we be conducted to Lord Pelester, at your convenience."

"Another?" one said. "Should we—"

"Silence." The corporal of the guard, a fiftyish man with metal rank tabs of green copper on the shoulders of his harness, had never taken his eyes off Toryn and his companions. "Perhaps. Quite perhaps. You travel on orders of the Guildmaster, yes?"

"Yes," Toryn said. "Given to me by him in person."

"Oh. And how is that old injury to his wrist?"

"Nonexistent," Toryn said, his sneer accompanied by a derisive snort. "That was the previous one. Guildmaster Yryn has a small scar under his lip, hidden by his beard—but that came from biting through it during the Ordeal. It was Eldren who had the bad wrist. The right wrist." He eyed the guard levelly. "And what else would you like to know about private matters concerning my Guild brothers?"

"No offense meant, none at all," the guard said, raising a palm in protest or acquiescence. "Just doing my job, Journeyman, just doing my job. You seek the Warrior? With hired help?" He eyed Jason, holding his gaze long enough to make it clear that he would not turn from a challenge, but not quite long enough to pose a challenge.

"Yes," Jason said. "His coin is as good as any other."

"And you are . . . ?"

Jason almost used Taren, a common name and his usual alias, but he didn't want Toryn to know his usual alias. "Festen of Wehnest," he said. "Called 'the Lucky.' " He jerked a thumb toward Ahira. "My dwarf companion: Denerrin of Endell."

The corporal looked suspicious. "I thought there was some sort of . . . arrangement between Endell and Holtun-Bieme."

Ahira snorted. "There was. I didn't like it. I left."

"And you work for humans now."

"They pay. I work." He patted at the pouch at his belt. "They don't, I walk."

He didn't glare at Jason, but there was something in his manner that made Jason think Ahira was irritated with him. Still, it had been the right move—on the off-chance that one of these knew anything about the Endell warrens, Ahira, who had lived there for a decade, could have given the right answer.

"You have objections to my companions?" Toryn asked, his voice low.

The guard's face broke into a smile that Jason decided was intended to be ingratiating. "Not at all, Master Toryn."

"Journeyman Toryn, if you please." _I don't need to put on airs,_ the sniff with which he punctuated the sentence said. "And are there standing orders regarding guildsmen presenting themselves?"

"Yes, we're to show you the hospitality of the town—"

"Then why do we sit here baking in the sun?" Toryn raised a finger, interrupting the start of the guard's protestations. "Lead us to Lord Pelester's keep, and see to our horses, and we'll forget all this impertinent questioning."

The corporal smiled as he shook his head. "That would do me no favor, young Journeyman—but I'll see to your horses and see you to the lord anyway."

"_In my house,_ he was," Lord Pelester raged, gesturing at the serving-girl to pour him more wine. He rose, holding up his hand to tell Toryn to keep his seat, not appearing to notice that he hadn't started to rise. "He sat under my roof, eating my food, and lay under my roof, in a bed of mine, with my favorite slave girl. In my house."

Jason and Ahira hadn't been offered seats or refreshment; they stood behind Toryn's chair, but at no particular position of attention: hired guards devoted to their duty, but not to the appearance of doing their duty. It all fit with their assumed roles, but Jason silently fumed, knowing that the slaver was enjoying lolling in a chair, a hot mug of tea, a longstemmed glass of inky wine, and a platter of sweetmeats at his elbow, while they stood hungry and thirsty.

His lordship had received them in a small study off the keep's great hall, a room whose walls were covered with oil paintings of previous lords in courageous poses—one over the dead body of an improbably small dragon, barely twice the size of a horse.

Jason hadn't had a lot of experience with a lot of dragons—just the one—but the creature looked too old to be so small. Was it a young one, or a small one, or had the artist simply shrunk the dragon to fit into a frame where a lord could pose heroically, the butt of his lance on the blood-soaked ground, one foot on the dragon's chest?

"In my house," Pelester repeated. He was a tall man, smooth complexion over thick cheekbones and massive jaw, peasant's bones wrapped in noble skin. He was dressed in silver and black that reminded Jason of Imperial livery; his fingers were bare of rings—in fact, he wore no jewelry save for a signet ring on a delicate-looking silver chain around his neck, and he incessantly, almost obscenely fondled the ring as he talked.

His glare fixed on Toryn. "He identified himself as a master of your Guild, and I had no reason to doubt him. It was hours after he was gone the next morning that Sensell, my slave-keeper, was found dead. And if I—" he waved the matter away. "If a spot of indigestion hadn't kept me alone in my own bed, I likely could have joined him."

Well, that explained the extra questioning by the guards. Mikyn had passed himself off as a Guild slaver, and gotten away with it, long enough to kill off Pelester's slave-handler.

Despite everything, it was all Jason could do not to smile. A slave-handler dead, and Toryn the slaver embarrassed. _Not bad, Mikyn._

"Well," Toryn said, "we're closer than we've been before. I'll ask for your hospitality tonight for myself, my horses, and my companions, and we'll pick up the trail in the morning."

"Granted, of course." Pelester dismissed the matter with a wave of his hand. "You may have a guest suite in the keep—"

"—and I'll need for my companions to sleep in

the outer room." Toryn spread his hands. "They're too devoted to me to allow me to close my eyes otherwise."

"That's hardly necessary here."

"We watch him." Ahira grunted. "He dies, we look bad. He lives, we get paid."

"Of course." Pelester nodded. "You'll dispatch a messenger when you've . . . dealt with him."

"It will be generally known, I promise you," Toryn said.

"That isn't good enough. I want to know, personally, that he's dead. Is there any part of that you don't understand?"

"As you wish it, of course," Toryn said. He sipped at his steaming mug of tea. "You have many slaves here?"

"Just a few. Mostly too old to do much more than help tenants plant their crops. Nothing like it was in my father's time. Most of my own fields are tilled by tenants; I dislike sharing the crop, but it's just too expensive these days to buy labor; cheaper to hire it." He eyed the serving girl. "On the other hand, we do have good crops these days, and that pays for some diversions." Pelester beckoned the serving girl over and pulled her to a sitting position on the arm of his chair, one hand resting possessively on her hip.

She was about Jason's age, slender rather than slim, and the thinness of the creamy cotton shift, belted tightly at the waist to accentuate the swell of her breasts, made it clear that it was her only garment. Her hair was black as coal, framing a delicate face with full, red lips that parted for just a moment, a hint of pink tongue playing at the corner of her mouth.

She smiled and nestled closer to Pelester; he patted her hip in dismissal, and she returned to the sideboard, straightening cups and refilling a boiling copper kettle in its rack over a small brazier.

"Just a few of the household servants, these days, like Marnea, here," Pelester said. "My treat for last year's tax surplus."

"Hmm." It was all Jason could do not to snarl at the way Toryn eyed her professionally. "Klimosian?"

"Indeed." Pelester's eyebrows raised. "Most mistake her for a Salkosian, what with her hair and coloration."

A thin smile. "Salkos hasn't had a famine for eleven years; Klimos' swamp-rice crop failed six years ago, and when they need money, they tend to start by selling daughters who are just barely rounding."

"Quite." Pelester shrugged the matter aside. "Would you like her for the night?"

Marnea's back stiffened, for just a moment, and then she returned to her work. She had been passed around before, it seemed, but she was not used to it.

Jason's fist clenched. The right thing to do was to draw his sword, announce who he was, and hack his way out through the local lord.

But he couldn't do the right thing, not here, not now.

A thin smile crossed Toryn's face. "Not I, but I think it's been too long since Festen's been properly serviced; he's off his feed, and overly tense. Have her sent to him later."

"Indeed," Pelester said, "it has been too long; he reddens at the thought."

"I think we embarrass him; and he's too useful in a fight to anger permanently. Let us change the subject."

Jason could, at the moment, have gladly strangled the slaver.

"What was that all about?" Jason hissed as soon as the old majordomo, with a bow, had closed the heavy door to their suite behind them. It was a standard sort of arrangement: an outer sitting room, a low couch and chair on the carpeting near the open window; the curtained, arched doorway in the center of the far wall left room for two sleeping pallets in front of it, so that a noble—or slaver—could have his guards sleep across his doorway.

Toryn tapped a finger to his ear. "Keep your voice low, young Festen," he said, quietly, gently, the violence of his glare belying the tone of his voice. "It was only common courtesy." He leaned close to Jason, his breath offensively warm in Jason's ear as he whispered. "And, besides, while you wouldn't have let me have her, one of us ought to talk to her. Had you been listening, you would have heard Pelester telling us he lent her to Mikyn. Perhaps something unexpected slipped out between the sheets. That which slips one way may slip again, eh?" he asked, his smile offensively broad. He gestured to the room beyond. "Denerrin and I will sleep there," he said, raising his voice, "while you can spend the night . . . investigating local customs." Toryn smiled.

Jason was beginning to dislike that smile more than he would have thought possible.

The slaver executed an overelaborate bow. "In the meantime, I learned as an apprentice to get what sleep I can when I can; I will bid the two of you a good night."

Jason watched his back as the slaver disappeared through the curtains.

He turned to Ahira. "Share with me your thoughts, if it please you," he said in Dwarvish, his voice pitched low enough that he wasn't worried about being overheard, even if the locals did understand the Moderate People's language.

"Cloudy." Ahira shrugged. "My thoughts, young son of my friend, are scattered and confused, and they're cloudy." The dwarf smiled, as though at a private joke, before he plopped himself down on the couch and began removing his boots. "I don't know," he said, switching back to Erendra. "I don't doubt the geas—not if cast by Vair the Uncertain and vouched for by Nareen the Glassmaker—but it's just a spell." Blunt fingers removed a boot, then gently rubbed at the gnarled toes.

"I don't know what you mean."

"Magic is, well, literal," Ahira said in English, his voice low. "It doesn't have a subtext—it doesn't mean anything beyond what it explicitly promises. Toryn isn't our partner, he doesn't work from the same principles we do. We can count on him not to slip a knife in our back, and with the geas we can count on him not to sit silent while somebody else does it—but we can't count on him to think seven steps ahead to prevent somebody else from doing it, the way Walter would." The dwarf shook his head. "And he reeks of some sort of unmentioned agenda, and that scares me." Ahira pulled off a second boot. "I wish Walter were here; trickiness is his sort of thing, not mine." He looked at Jason long and hard.

*I wish I had your father here instead of you,* he might as well have said.

The dwarf tossed his boots toward the arched, curtained doorway, then padded after them across the carpet. "G'night, Jason. Find out what you can."

And then he was alone.

\* \* \*

There was something more than vaguely obscene about all this, Jason decided, as he kicked off his own boots, then loosened his belt and lay back on his bedding, the back of his head pillowed on his hands.

His first time had been with a serving girl, name of Elarrah, but that was hardly the same thing. She was a maid in the castle at Holtun-Bieme, an orphan left behind in the war, several years older than he was, and he was the Heir—they had struck up a friendship that had ended with her sneaking into his room at night, every now and then. Nothing complicated about it, nothing compulsory about it, nothing obscene about it, nothing risky about it—she visited the Spider twice a year, she explained, and was hardly going to keep her job if she angered Jason's father, and could hardly find herself a husband with the Heir's bastard swelling her belly, on her hip, or tagging along behind.

She had married a corporal in the house guard, he had heard—lucky man.

He took another pull at the bottle of wine.

The truth was that it had been too long for him and that, as Walter Slovotsky put it, the terminal hornies was the only terminal disease that you don't die of, and that Marnea was nicely shaped, and that he was tired of waking up with—

The door creaked open, and she was there,

carrying a tray in one hand, a shrouded candle-stick in the other.

"Good evening," he said.

Her eyes didn't meet his as she set the the tray down on a low stand: it held a small platter of cheese and meatrolls, and a tall bottle, along with two glasses.

"And a good evening to you." She knelt by the tray, dressed only in a short patterned wrap-around dress, fastened with a tuck at the swell of her breasts and a slip-knotted belt at the waist. As she knelt, the hem rode high up on her thighs. They were very nice thighs.

"I think you'll like this. It's a chilled Elsinian." She poured him a glass of wine, and then an-other. "Do you mind? There's no rush unless you feel one—I'm yours for the night." She moved next to him, handing him a glass. Her fingers played with the knot of her belt, and her head was tilted to one side.

"Did Mikyn get the same treatment?" He sipped at the wine. Very nice, and almost icy cold, but not cold enough to draw away a vague taste of vanilla and honey, or a distant flowery whiff that could almost have been a perfume.

"He . . . yes," she said. "Yes. We spent most of the night talking, strangely enough."

"What would you and a Guild slaver have to talk about?" he asked.

She started for a moment, then shrugged. "Various things."

_Bullshit_. There was something wrong here, and he couldn't quite put his finger on it.

He nibbled at a meatroll. Different than what U'len made— less garlic, he decided, and none of it wild—but in some ways almost as good. Another swig of wine cleared his palate.

She bent over and kissed him, her lips warm against his, her mouth parted, her tongue warm and wet against his. He reached for her belt—

No. This wasn't right. It wasn't playful, like it had been with Elarrah, or intense and almost frighteningly fierce, the way it was with Janie. It was somehow dirty and shameful, and not something that the son of Karl Cullinane would have done—

_And it wasn't something that Mikyn would have done, either._

Not after the way Mikyn had been mistreated, when he was only a boy, before Karl and his raiders had freed him and his father. There was no reason to believe that Mikyn couldn't function with a woman—but not an owned one, not one with no choice, one under compulsion of whip and iron.

"Mikyn." He pulled back from her. "He told you who he was, didn't he?"

Her eyes grew wide, and she paled, visibly, even in the candlelight. Damn, damn, damn.

"No, no, nothing of the sort," she said. "I was fooled, too. He—"

"—pulled away from you, just like I did, only more so." Jason knew that he shouldn't be thinking out loud. But all the bells were ringing in his head, and he knew with an awful clarity what had happened with Mikyn.

"Because he couldn't take you, not under compulsion, because that is to Mikyn the most horrible thing that can happen to somebody, whether it's a little boy or a grown woman."

Her headshake was almost hysterical. "No, please."

Idiot. She wasn't thinking things through. Jason couldn't help doing just that. What would Mikyn have done if he'd found himself exposed so? Remember that he was crazy, that he was on a rogue rampage, killing off slave-owners right and left—but remember that he was also functioning well enough to pass himself off as a traveling farrier or a Guild slaver.

Mikyn was not a drooling idiot; he was devious and he was clever.

"He promised he'd come back for you," Jason said. Mikyn had been a slave, and had grown up around former slaves; he knew full well that there was not necessarily more virtue to be found among the owned than the owners. Marnea would be too likely to talk, and would have to be silenced. There would be two ways to silence her:

with death, or with a promise, a believed promise.

She was inching for the door, and at his look turned the slow motion into a quick scrabble. Jason grabbed her by an ankle and pulled her back, wrapping one arm around to pin her arms to the side and fastening a hand over her mouth.

What was true for Mikyn was true for Jason. There were two ways to silence her.

"Stop it," he hissed, vaguely embarrassed at the way she had stopped struggling. It wasn't just that he was that much stronger than her; it was that she had been taught not to struggle. "I'm Jason Cullinane," he said. "And I'll honor his promise to you."

He hadn't thought her eyes could get any wider. She relaxed in his arms, and he slowly, gingerly removed his hand from her mouth.

"There you have it," he said. "My life's in your hands; all you have to do is tell who I am, and I'm sure Pelester will be grateful. But do you think he'd free you?"

She shook her head.

"Is that what you want? Freedom, and a place to go?"

She nodded.

"Good," he said. "We'd better go wake the others."

* * *

It was hard to tell who was less thrilled about being woken up from sleep, Toryn or Ahira, although it was close.

Ahira scowled. "I saw no need to complicate matters," he said in Dwarvish. "Had I seen such, I could have complicated them myself."

"I thank you for your observation," Jason responded in the same language, then switched to Erendra. Dwarvish wasn't very good at expressing irritation; the Moderate People weren't much on being irritated.

"What did you expect me to do?" Jason asked the dwarf. He didn't mind the constant sense that whatever he did was inadequate—well, maybe he did—but he surely didn't have to stand for criticism when there was no alternative.

"Is this supposed to be a trick question?" Ahira snorted. "Couldn't you say you were too tired? I think you've been hanging out with Walter too much—even men are allowed to say no, every now and then."

"I wish you'd mentioned that before," Jason said.

"I didn't think I had to."

Jason was about to say something else when he was interrupted by Toryn's laugh. Dressed only in a white silken robe belted tightly at the waist, Toryn lay back on his bedding, propped on one elbow. "Well, it could be worse, although I hardly know how. If you hadn't exposed us, all we would have had to do was tell Lord Pelester that she had gotten more out of Mikyn than a quick poke, and let him ask her, gently, gently, what she knew." He glanced at where Marnea sat in the corner, looking to Jason every now and then for assurance.

Jason tried not to snarl. "I did as I thought best."

"So you did," Toryn said, his expression making it clear that he thought Jason's best failed being good enough by a large measure. He turned to Marnea. "Did he arrange a rendezvous with you, or did he promise to ride back for you?"

"I'll tell you," she said, "after I'm away from here."

Toryn chuckled. "Done. I'll buy you from Pelester, and we'll sell you, say, in—"

"No," Jason said. "We don't sell people."

"Oh, Jason Cullinane," Toryn said with a chuckle. "You may have it your way. Fine; so we'll buy her and free her. I'll tell Pelester in the morning: I've taken a fancy to you, and offer—" He stopped himself and shook his head. "No, that might not work. You're really rather a pretty little thing, and he might well want you more than any money I could credibly spend. And that would mean, if he turned me down, that when you disappeared, we would be the suspects." He tilted his head to one side.

It was Ahira's turn to smile. "Giving the Guild a bad reputation. Such a pity."

"Which is why, friend Ahira, I won't offer to buy her. Even assuming that I don't fear having Pelester's men on my trail." He reached a hand out and lifted her chin. She didn't resist; she was far too used to being handled. "Pity. And now, knowing what she does, we can hardly leave her behind, to trade her knowledge about us for, perhaps, some promise of better treatment, eh? Or freedom, even?" He tapped her on the nose. "Do remember, Marnea, that owners often lie to slaves about such."

He let go of her chin and dismissed the problem with a wave of a hand and a yawn that seemed as much from boredom as from sleepiness. "Well, I'll leave it in the hands of these two; freeing slaves is their business. Mine, for the moment, is resting my eyes." He disappeared back into the sleeping room, returning momentarily with his blankets and his scabbarded sword. He spread the blankets in front of the closed door and lay down, his sword next to him, his careful look at Marnea a warning that hardly needed to be said out loud. He pulled a blanket over himself and closed his eyes. "Wake me in the morning, unless you figure to make a run for it tonight."

Jason turned to Ahira.

"I . . . may have a plan," the dwarf said. "Let

me think on it for a while." He tossed a pair of blankets toward Marnea, then kicked Jason's blankets toward the sleeping room. "You get some sleep."

It was sometime around dawn that she came to him.

His father would have woken completely at the slightest touch, but Jason floundered around before he realized that he wasn't alone in bed, and that warm fingers were working at the buttons of his trousers; then for a moment, on the edge of sleep, he thought he was back in Biemestren, and with Elarrah.

He thought of pushing her away, or of explaining that they really would rescue her anyway, but her mouth was warm and wet and alive on his, and her hair smelled of soap and flowers, and knowing, practiced fingers were easing him out of his clothing, and he decided that not only wasn't he as noble as his father had been, but that he didn't give a damn, and reached for her.

# 9

# Home

Home is the place where, when you have to go there, they have to take you in.

—ROBERT FROST

When arguing with friends or family, the worst position you can be in is when you're right and they know you are. It limits your ability to plead guilty to a lesser, as they know you don't really mean it.

—WALTER SLOVOTSKY

Almost twenty years changes a lot.

When I first saw the valley of Varnath, as the elves call it, it was the dark green of forest and grasslands, broken only by silver threads of streams running down from the mountains into the central lake. Brightly colored birds twittered in the trees, and butterflies and the smell of flowers filled the air.

At least, that's the way I remember it. I don't remember as clearly the ache of my tender butt from too many days in the saddle, or the way my jerkin kept rubbing against the spot where some bug the size of my left nut had sucked out a quart of blood, leaving behind God's Own Mosquito Bite.

Then again, which would you choose to have close to the top of your mind? The beauty and the pleasure, or the pain and the itch?

Now, what had been grasslands below was a plaid patchwork of fields, mostly in shades of brown, separated by only strips of forest. Sort of like the valley had been given a bikini wax. Lines of power cable stretched from the forest at the foot of the falls, running both into the town of Home itself and out toward the foothills. Thinner wires ran out toward the nearest farms—having a telegraph handy was more important, perhaps, and certainly a lot cheaper, than electricity.

Over in Engineer Territory, by the lowest of the foothills, near what we called the Batcave (Karl and I used to break into a little tune that went "_dah_-dah-_dah_-dah-_dah_-dah-_dah_," in a joke that even the other Other Siders never found all that funny), a cluster of factories belched foul, sulphurous smoke into the air, and as the warm air currents over a fallow field gave Ellegon some added (and in my opinion, unneeded) lift, they brought with them the smell of rotting manure.

Which may have been wonderful for next year's wheat and potatoes, but did little for my nostrils.

Progress sometimes stinks.

Still, the lake was clean and clear and blue, and looked inviting, as the dragon circled down toward the town square. Lou knew better than to use the lake as a dumping ground; doesn't take long to turn a small lake into a large, smelly cesspool.

I lowered myself to the solid ground, although as always after a long dragonback ride, it felt just a little jellyish under my feet, and it took me a minute to be able to stand straight instead of like a drunk on his third tankard.

It gets harder to travel as I get older; I felt like I had been either on the road for weeks or buried for days—it's hard to tell the difference—and am sure that I looked it.

Adahan, on the other hand, ran his neatly manicured fingers through his hair, gave a quick tug to his combination pistol/swordbelt, and tucked the ends of his tunic into his trousers, looking disgustingly fresh as he hoisted his bag to his shoulder.

"Well, where do we go?" he asked.

I didn't know; I'd sort of expected to be met.

*Understandable. Nobody around here has anything else to do except greet Walter Slovotsky, and ask if they may be of service.*

Bren Adahan smirked, and I resolved to have a few short words with the dragon about the nature and practice of private conversation.

*And what would you do if I told you to stuff it? Refuse to beg me to help you next time?*

A small troop of men was exiting from a low brick building next to the grainery, and a stream of schoolchildren was already, well, streaming out of the doors of the schoolhouse toward the square. Voices called out greetings—

—for the dragon.

*What did you expect? A parade?* He turned his huge saurian head toward the approaching children. *Stand back, please, until I'm unloaded —you don't want to get in the way.*

One of the men—Evain, I think his name was; he had been on Daven's raiding team at one point—called out a greeting to me, but another glared at him and grumbled something about work to be done.

It took only a couple of minutes for the men to unload Ellegon and unstrap his rigging. The dragon, surrounded by at least three dozen children ranging in age from about six to about sixteen, carefully lumbered off toward the lake, their shouts of glee occasionally interrupted by a skyward gout of fire and a mental caution.

*Benric, if you keep pushing Katha, I can promise you you'll be last in line for a dive, and— Menten, be patient, yes, I'll swim out with you. Karl, you can't climb up on me when I'm walking—it's too tricky.*

That last gave me a start, but I kept it out of

my face. There were more than a couple children named after Karl, and even a Walter or two. There was even a chubby-cheeked blond girl, her hair done up in a complex braid that spoke of her mother's Aersten ancestry, named Tennetty, although it would be hard to think of a person looking less like Ten.

I looked over at Bren.

He shrugged. "Me, too."

Just as well. I wouldn't want to be the only person spooked.

A horse-drawn flatbed wagon had been pulled up to the pile of bags and boxes, and Bren and I joined in the loading. It was good to be doing something as simple and stable as lifting a bag onto the weathered boards, but with eight of us working, it was only a matter of a couple of minutes until the driver released the brake, and with a click of his tongue and a twitch of the reins, sent the wagon rattling down the road.

Two figures emerged from the dark of the brick house, one dwarf, one human, the dwarf moving at a quick but comfortable hobble despite the fact that his right leg, from just above the knee down, was a knobby piece of wood terminating in a brass ferrule.

"Nehera, Petros," I called out.

The scars that crisscrossed Nehera's lined face, reminders of whippings he had received long ago, had faded almost to invisibility—or, more accurately, taken on the permanent just-this-side-of-sunburn red that years over his forge had given the rest of his face, forearms and hands. His treetrunk-thick forearms were heat-reddened beneath the short, dark hair, save in a few dozen spots where white scars told of a small spattering of hot metal.

But he stood with his back straight, and his crooked-toothed smile broadened as he extended a hand. "Walter Slovotsky—'tis good to see you, years though it's been." Idly, he used the brass tip of his peg leg to kick a small stone out of the road and into the strip of trees surrounding the square.

The years had been kind to the dwarf, albeit not to Petros, whose face was too deeply lined for somebody ten years younger than me. There was a sort of watery look to his eyes, and when he stopped in front of me, he just glared, which didn't seem to stretch his face into an unusual state. His beard was still scraggly, although that was the only thing that looked young about him. He looked more like a jury than a welcoming committee. "Lou wants to see you," he said. "He's waiting; let's go."

"So what's the problem?" I asked. "Why the cold shoulder?"

"Bast is back," he said, his words paced evenly, carefully. "He says that you've given away the secret of gunpowder."

"Oh," I said. I would have rather said *I did not, and how dare you suggest that I would,* but not only wouldn't that have been true, but I wouldn't have been able to get away with it.

Nehera smiled at me, but Nehera always smiled at everyone.

I first met Louis Riccetti as a freshman, in a music appreciation class that he was taking to fulfill a distribution requirement and that I was taking because I, well, appreciated music. He had been balding even then—well, to be fair, his hair was thinning and his hairline retreating—his eyes were well on their way to a permanent squint, and his shoulders were tending toward the hunched. He was nineteen, I think, but looked at least five, maybe ten years older. From the pocket protector down to his white socks with brown shoes, he looked like a classic computer geek—although he in fact wasn't; he didn't have much use for computers.

Appearances can be deceiving, even when they're not trying to be.

To a background of Bach and Beethoven, Ravel and Rameau, Mozart and Mendelssohn, Puccini and Prokofiev, we had struck up a distant friendship mainly based on my having spent one summer as an apprentice blacksmith at Sturbridge Village—being a smith is a tough, hot, sweaty job; being a part-time apprentice smith a hundred steps from a locker room complete with high-pressure shower and a Coke machine isn't—and his interest in metalworking of all sorts, which had eventually led to my invitation to a gaming session with Professor Deighton . . .

But that was another country, and another time.

We were all getting older. The fringe of hair that rimmed his scalp was a dingy gray with occasional bits of black, and although his arms and legs were skinny, he had developed a permanent potbelly that pushed against the buttons of his shirt as he pushed his chair back from his desk and folded his hands in his lap, eyeing me with rather more appraisal than approval.

"Greetings, Mr. Mayor," I said, trying for a light tone.

"Hello, Walter. Greetings, Baron Adahan," he said, with a nod and a smile that was clearly intended for Adahan, although the smile was hardly big enough to bother with. "Have a seat."

The shades had been drawn, and the room was dark. On his desk, crowned with a bleached parchment lampshade, an electric light glowed, although the desk had been placed so that more than enough light would stream in through the mottled-glass window for any sort of paperwork. Lou was showing off.

"You want to talk about the gunpowder," I said.

His lips pursed for a moment, and then he nodded. "Yeah. That would be a good start. I want to give you a fair hearing—Bast said you gave out the secret."

"Well, yes, I did, and I did it in order to save not only my own life, and Bast's and Kenda's— but Ahira's, Tennetty's, Jason's, and Andy's."

He was toying with a smooth stone, a paperweight or something, that he had taken from his desktop. "He mentioned that," Lou said, as though that factor had already been weighed in my defense and found to be negligible. "He also said that you had a chance to . . . back out of the problem."

Yes, I perhaps could have had Erol Lyneian and all the crew aboard his ship killed, but the rest of us wouldn't have been able to sail it, not in the rocky waters near Ehvenor, not to the hill overlooking the gleaming city, where the Three waited . . .

Without that—without us—Faerie would have continued to leak out into reality, and the trickle of strange, magical creatures would have become a full-fledged flood.

I hadn't known that at the time, though. I had known that Andy said we needed to get closer to Ehvenor, and I had trusted her.

And I'd had little appetite for a fight anyway, not after the way we had almost been killed in

Brae, and maybe part of that was because I was slowing down.

"Maybe," I said. "But I was there and you weren't, and it was my call, not yours." I shrugged. "I guess I could have waited until they started sawing away on me, or on Andy or any of the rest, but I didn't. It was a nice bit of strategy— split up two allies quite neatly, and got us out of there intact." I snorted. "And, by the way, put an end to a local lord who stuck a bunch of your engineers up on poles to die of exposure."

He took a deep breath and let it out. "Which doesn't make it right, does it?"

I could have argued, I could have pointed out that the secret was going to get out eventually, and what with Home and the Holtun-Bieme Empire preparing to switch over to smokeless powder and sealed ammunition, it wasn't like I'd given away the store. There had been the too-expensive slaver rifles around for years, after all.

And I could have pointed out that the secret no more belonged to Lou than it did to me, that I knew fifteen-three-and-two as well as he did, even if he had grown to think of it as his property, to be shared with only his most inner circle of engineers.

His eyes rested on mine long enough to make me wish I knew of a side exit. A quick leap over the desk, a slap on the throat to silence him long enough for me to deal with Petros, and—

—and I'd still have Nehera to handle, although the dwarf had never been quick-witted, but—

*Ellegon? You wouldn't happen to be ready for a quick getaway, would you?*

*Probably not.* The dragon's mental voice was laconic and indifferent. *I'm playing. Leave me alone.*

—without Ellegon, I'd still be in the valley, having just attacked Lou, the Engineer, who was surrounded by a bunch of disciples only a little more devoted to him than the Apostles were to their Teacher.

Ever wonder why you don't see a lot of little kids named Judas Iscariot?

He smiled thinly. "Well, I guess we'll let it go, given that I don't see any other good choice."

I felt Bren Adahan relax just a trifle, and realized that he had been keyed up, ready to move, to follow my lead, presumably—or, conceivably, to rap me on the head and hand me over to Lou.

Save it for later. "You know what I've always liked about you, Lou?" I asked.

"What?"

"That having me killed never's seemed to you to be a good choice."

He didn't smile at the pleasantry. I would have said something like *What are you, an audience or a jury?*, but under the circumstances . . .

"What do you need?" he asked.

"For tonight? Food for four—Bren and I are

hungry—two beds, and all the news that any-body's heard about the Warrior. For tomorrow, five of Daven's best trackers, supplies, money, and guns."

"Guns," he said.

Among old friends, it's not always the things you say, but sometimes the things you don't say.

He didn't say: after giving away the secret of black powder, something I've been saving for as long as possible, you're asking me to put revolvers in your hands, and that's asking a lot, Walter, probably more than I should give you.

And I didn't say: look, Lou, I'm not Karl, and I'm not the world's best swordsman, and I'm go-ing in harm's way with Bren Adahan at my side, not Karl and Ahira and Tennetty and Chak, and I need every bit of edge I can get, and a repeating handgun would be a big one.

And he didn't say: the Therranji want to annex us, and to keep them at bay we need an edge, something scary enough that they won't push hard and turn it into war, and right now, smoke-less powder is a big part of that, too important to be risked on the likes of you.

And I didn't say: I know. And I know we're al-ways going to disagree on that, but I'm asking you anyway.

And he didn't say: and since you know too much about the making of it, and since I know you'll spend information instead of your life, I can't even let you leave here, much less give you a sample of a repeating handgun.

No. We didn't say anything. But he looked at me for a long time, and then he pulled open a drawer in his desk, pulled out a wooden box, and, removing a keychain from around his neck, opened the box with a small key.

Inside the box, under an oilcloth that Lou pulled aside, on a bed of blue satin, like some sort of jewels, two pistols lay, not quite touching, nested together like a yin and yang—unless you prefer a more earthy metaphor; I always do— surrounded by a circle of half-moon clips, each of which held three shiny brass cartridges.

The pistols weren't black powder flintlocks, but revolvers, more blackened than blued, the barrel length maybe four inches, the grips polished bone, carefully checkered for a good grip. The sights were low and rounded, unlikely to catch on clothing. Not exactly pocket pistols, but easy enough to conceal underneath a tunic, or even strap to an ankle if your trousers were blousy enough. They looked a bit strange to me, but I quickly figured it out—they had been made smooth, with no sharp edges to catch on clothing as you tried to draw. Even the hammer spur was abbreviated and rounded.

Lou knew what he was doing, at least when it came to making things.

He picked one up and idly opened the cylinder, revealing the shiny brass heads of six cartridges, then slowly, gently, closed the cylinder. "If you flick it shut, the way they used to on TV," he said, "you're pretty quickly going to knock the cylinder out of alignment. Screws the accuracy all to hell. Always push the cylinder closed." He tucked it into his belt, then picked up the other, opened it, showed it, closed it. "This one's mine; the other's yours."

Petros was on his feet. *"No.* You're not."

Petros might as well have not been talking, and when he opened his mouth again, Nehera reached over and laid a flipper of a hand on Petros' arm.

"No safety switch," Lou went on, "but the hammer is blocked from the firing pin unless the trigger's pulled back. It will not fire, even cocked, if the trigger isn't held back, so you can keep a round under the hammer. There's only a few of these," he said, "and they're trickier to make than they look; the rest of your party will have to do with Benden's breechloading flintlocks—paper cartridges," he said. "Faster than muzzleloaders, but not quite up to these. There's a target range out on the East road, and the armorer will issue you as much ammunition as you want," Lou said. "I'd say go through at least two boxes; carry two with you. Save your brass. You can have one of the apprentices clean the gun for you."

The right thing to do was nod silently, but nobody told my mouth that. "I can clean up after myself."

"Yeah." Lou put the gun back in the box, closed the top, turned the key, carefully removed the key and slapped it on top of the box. He slid it across his desk to me, then put his hands on the surface of his desk and pushed himself to his feet. He came around the desk, a hand outstretched.

When I took it, it felt stronger than it used to be.

When I was younger, I used to think that it was something special just between the six of us—me, Ahira, Karl, Andy, Doria, and Lou—because we were Other Siders, trapped in a world we had never made, or because we were such special people. It took me years to realize that it was the years, the years that we had shared not just the big things—sweat and tears, blood and pain, food and shelter, the birth of kids, the death of mutual friends—but the little things: the idle conversation at the end of a long day, the ongoing argument over whether a gelding or a mare made for a better saddlehorse.

It was the little things that were important, and the little things I really missed with Kirah. I've lost too many people I care about, and sometimes I didn't realize how much I cared until they were gone.

And I hadn't realized how important Lou was to me, just personally, until he said, Don't make me wrong, but he didn't need to say it with words; he said it with a smile that spoke of trust, and more important, of friendship.

We were friends again.

"I like the lightbulb," I said. "Impressive."

"Yeah." He grinned. "Thought you might."

There are parts of all this that you can have for the asking: the mud, the blood, and the crud, for a start. The separation from the family—how many nights have I been robbed of tucking my baby daughter in for the night? The road food and the fear—both taste lousy in my mouth.

But there are compensations: like a lake shore near a stream inlet, where the soft grasses ran not only up to the edge of the lake but into it, and beneath the cold water were soft and pleasant against my feet and between my toes; like warm afternoon air carrying with it the mellow tang of sunbaked grasses and distant cheery shouts from where, hidden beyond the small island placed off-center in the lake, children played and splashed with a dragon, an occasional gout of flame reaching skyward to punctuate some mental caution; like a box containing two pistols holding down my clothing on the shoreline.

A few feet away, a few feet farther out, beyond the spot where the gentle slope of the lake dropped off to God-knows-how-deep, Bren Adahan was treading water—for the exercise, I guess.

He tossed his head to clear the water out of his eyes, sending bright drops arcing high into the sunlight.

"Blood and dust tomorrow, but we swim and soak today, eh, Walter Slovotsky?"

"Something like that, Baron," I said. "Best to put off some suffering, when you can."

Professional trick: when you've got something serious to worry about—say, getting involved in a chase for a former companion who has gone both crazy and ballistic—and there's nothing useful that worrying about that will do, pick something relatively minor and worry about *that,* instead.

It won't do you any good, mind, but you won't feel as bad.

I thought about the hell I'd be in for when I got home, from Andy. I'd said I'd take her out on the road with me, and I would—but not now, not for this. Bad enough to be chasing after Jason and Ahira; worse to be looking for Mikyn; best not to involve her in me fleeing from the Emperor, even though my guess was that he would want to let it all drop rather than letting me defy him so openly. (Take it out on my family? Are you kidding? Nobody in court would even suggest it. Somebody raises their hand to my family, they don't just have Walter Slovotsky cutting it off: add Ahira, Ellegon, and Lou, for starters.)

There wouldn't be any hell to pay from Aeia, or the girls. Aeia would just cock her head to one side and smile, and maybe hold me a little too tight, but I wouldn't mind. Janie and Doranne were used to having me around, and to having me gone—they'd be happy to see me, but neither of them would have missed me the way I missed them.

I heard distant hoofbeats and counted four horses, as I casually felt at the scabbard still strapped to my calf, and closed my eyes for a moment to be sure I could recall the spot on the island where I'd stashed a getaway kit some years back.

But it wasn't anything to worry about—just a couple of pretty young, more than vaguely pretty young women in Engineer jeans and flannel workshirts, each leading a spare horse. The taller, slightly blonder of the two girls tossed a pile of towels to the grass and swung a long leg over the saddle, dismounting prettily. I guess I imprinted early on young women in tight jeans, and the high heels of her riding boots gave an unusually nice line to her legs.

"Walter Slovotsky?" she called out.

Bren jerked a thumb at me. "Him. My name's Bren."

She made a moue. "Yes, Baron. I've heard. I'm Barda; she's Arien. We're journeymen. The Engineer said that if we brought you some towels, fed you enough supper, and asked you real prettily, you might be persuaded to talk about internal combustion engines."

I smiled at Adahan, as though to say, *I won't tell on you if you don't tell on me,* and he chuckled and spread his hands.

"Anything's possible," I said. "After you join us for a swim."

Her smile broadened. It was a pretty smile. Not as pretty as Aeia's, mind, but it was much, much closer. "Well, I thought you'd never ask."

She was already unbuttoning her shirt as she kicked off her boots, and after a quick hesitation, Arien followed her lead.

It's always interesting to watch pretty girls undress.

As I say, the work does have its compensations.

The dream is always the same:

*We're trying to make our escape from Hell, millions of us streaming across the hot rocks, while behind us the volcano rises immensely large, spewing demons and lava with equal vigor. Sometimes it's hard to tell the difference—ahead, a glowing red crack in the rock spews forth what at first looks like a blob of lava, but the blob gathers itself together and flows uphill, like an amoeba, except faster, fast enough to engulf one poor bastard who barely has time enough to get a scream out before the molten rock flows over his head, his hair burning until it disappears in the roiling surface.*

Up ahead, Lou Riccetti, wearing a fireman's coat, but his balding head bare as always, is out in front of a bunch of fire trucks, directing the men of Company 23 as the water from their hoses holds both lava and demons at bay.

But one of the trucks is unmanned, and there's a gap in their line that needs filling.

"Not exactly our kind o' war, eh, Bull?" His smile threatens to split his broad face in two, but Charley Beckwith's Southern drawl is firmly intact as he and Bull Simons grab a hose and fumble with it before it stiffens as it fills.

Simons chuckles. "Since when did that ever stop either of us?" he shouts back as old Jonas Salk steps in to help steady the hose, rewarded by a quick grin from Simons.

I'm hardly surprised to see Sister Berthe of Toulouse—the nun we used to call "Sister Birth of the Blues"—lunge for a hose that's gotten away from some others, even though she's not able to steady it until Jimmy Stewart lends a hand. Then again, that was the way Sister Berthe was—when they retired her from St. Olaf's, she went to work as a teacher's aide in an inner city school, saying that at least until she couldn't see to read, she'd teach children how to read.

But he is there again. Past where Karl and Andy, both of them old and white-haired, take their places between an ancient Tennetty and a fat, withered Buddha, past where Golda Meir stands argu-

*ing with Teddy Roosevelt about who is and isn't too old to be doing this, he stands with his band of sailors. His shoulders are huge, still, and his head is still erect. His skin is browned almost like leather by the sun, his hair and beard are bleached as white as his sailor's tunic, with the gold bands of royalty at its hem.*

*"Come," he calls to his companions, "there is work to be done, once more, once more. The hour grows late." His voice is strange, as though it's been broken, but has carried a long way.*

*I press through the crowd until I face him. "Who the hell are you?" I ask him.*

*His face is wrinkled, its creases deep and dark.*

*"Why," he says, "I'm nobody." And he smiles.*

*But I have to know who he is. It's important; I can live with the nightmares, with the waiting behind to face the demons, if only I know who he is.*

*"I'm Nobody," he repeats.*

*Then I wake up.*

I woke, an old Crosby, Stills and Nash song playing in the back of my head, the blankets under me wet with sweat.

The lamp over on the table next to the door was hooded, its wick trimmed—it was more of a nightlight than anything else. To wake up with somebody new wasn't uncomfortable, but to wake in a strange cabin in the dark would be a bit much.

The windows on both ends of the cabin were covered only with latticed shutters, letting enough cool night air flow through the cabin to chill me to the bone.

I slipped out of bed, rubbing at the odd scratch and bite mark, glad that she had clean fingernails. A towel hung on a hook near the window over the bed; I rubbed myself dry, and at least a little less cold, before I dressed silently, to avoid disturbing Arien.

I give good silent.

She was sort of curled up in the blankets, leaving one long, amazingly strong leg bare from toe to waist.

There was another set of surprises. I'd been flirting mainly with Barda, the more outgoing of the two, all evening, and expected to end the night with her, but the two of them had gone off for a private conversation, and it was Arien who had offered to show me the guest cabin I'd been assigned. While I wouldn't want it to get around, I didn't have the courage to ask whether it was because she had won or lost the coin toss.

There had been other surprises; I'd thought of her as quiet and shy. Live and learn, I always say.

I was still sleepy, but going back to bed right now would mean going back to dream. Better to get a bit of fresh air, and maybe see if the pantry was open over at the apprentice barracks.

I was reaching for the doorknob when I heard

Arien turn in the blankets. "Walter . . ." Her voice
was muffled by the pillow. ". . . if you're trying to
get away, shouldn't you be taking your gear?" she
asked.

"Yeah. Had a bad dream; I just need to clear
my head."

"Mmm. Wake me when you get back?"

"Sure," I said, lying. I'm not eighteen anymore;
I haven't been for more than twenty years. I just
needed to clear my head, and then sleep.

"Mmph."

I think she was asleep before I had the door
closed behind me.

The six cabins lined the street opposite the Engineer apprentice barracks, a two-story rough-
hewn wooden building that looked like somebody
had stacked a typical wooden house on top of a
log cabin.

Which is what had happened, actually.

It had started off as a storehouse, back before
we had a sawmill—we had just squared off a few
dozen logs, then built the house like we were
working with oversized Lincoln Logs (a dragon is
better than a crane, although a crane doesn't leave
toothmarks). Home building techniques—and, for
that matter, Home home-building techniques—
had improved dramatically over the years with the
addition of a sawmill, some freed carpenters, and
the ironworks.

But there was no reason to tear the old storehouse down, and when it was turned into the barracks, another story had just been piled on top of it. The kitchen was at the rear, and a lantern burned in the window.

Two kids, a skinny, acne-spattered boy of maybe fifteen and a round-faced girl, were working out some sort of math problem on a slate they'd set up on the table over by the door, and Petros was busying himself with a copper kettle on the boxy iron stove, feeding the stove a few pieces of scrap wood, then carefully poking at the fire with a wood-handled poker.

"Evening, Walter," he said evenly, no trace of hostility in his voice. "Tea?"

"Sure."

"Just another minute; it's almost hot enough."

The kids sort of mumbled something, then said a quick goodnight and left, taking their slate with them, when Petros looked pointedly toward the door.

"G'night, kids. Nice meeting you," I said.

Petros dumped a palmful of tea into a teapot, irised the stove's vents open a little, then adjusted the kettle down on the flat burner before finding a chair. He didn't seem to notice that he still had the poker in his hand, and I didn't seem to notice that I had the hilt of a knife concealed in mine.

Then he did look down at the poker in his

hand, and just hung it by its leather loop on a peg on the wall.

"Are you usually up this late?" I asked.

"Woman works from sun to sun, but the deputy mayor's job is never done," he said, setting a couple of mugs down on the counter.

"Not bad."

A quiet chuckle. "I listen to Lou a lot." He spooned a dripping teaspoonful of honey into each, then went to the stove for the hot water. "Probably more than anybody ever listened to anybody else. Learned a lot from him, but I didn't learn everything I know from him." It occurred to me that his first move would be to try to splash me with it, and that my move would be to protect my eyes and let the rest of my skin look out for itself. Nail him with the knife, then raise a cry.

But he just poured the steaming water into the porcelain teapot, set the kettle back down next to the stove, and brought the teapot and the mugs over to the table.

"I figured part of my job was to have a word or two with you before you leave in the morning," he said, as though it hadn't been a full minute since either of us spoke, "and I also figured that you'll be on your way early."

"So, have your word."

He nodded, slowly. "It's simple. Lou's retiring from the mayor's job next year. Says he wants to spend more time in the shop, the lab, and his study. I've got the Engineer vote, and enough of Samalyn's farmer faction that the job's mine if I want it."

"I guess congratulations are in order."

He went on as though he hadn't heard me: "I've been working toward this for years now, and for more reasons than I care to go into with the likes of you, I want it."

"You, like, want me to pass out campaign literature?"

"What I want is you to be absent. What I want is no Walter Slovotsky deciding that he's getting too old to be running around saving the world, and that he ought to settle down and relieve Lou of a job Lou never really wanted, with a few young women engineers to keep him warm on cold winter nights."

I could have said something like _that had never occurred to me,_ but the truth won't always set you free, or even be believed. "And in return I get to walk out that door alive?"

"No. No threat. I'll not end the night with my throat cut, and the dragon to swear that I threatened you before you bravely defended yourself." He snickered. "No. I'm a farmer and a politician, Walter. I'll not go hand-to-hand with you. I'm not threatening you; I'm just telling you to back off. No showing up unexpectedly around election time. No sudden withdrawals of all of your gold deposits to see what that does to the local economy. And no spilling of the secret of making smokeless powder just to see what interesting things it'll stir up, the way you did with black powder. I don't care if your last years are boring; I don't want any unnecessary excitement here."

"Would you take my word on it?"

"No." He poured tea into both mugs, then set the teapot down and sat back, gesturing at me to take my pick. He shook his head. "I'm not asking you, Walter Slovotsky. I'm just telling you how it is. Drink your tea, go back to your cabin, and in the morning get gone, and stay away from my home."

The lantern was still dimly lighting the cabin when I got back, and Arien was still asleep as I quickly undressed and slid into bed next to her.

Things change, over the years. I had helped to build this place, and make it live, but it wasn't my home anymore. Just another place to visit, or not.

I lay on my back, my head pillowed on the palms of my hands, and tried to sleep.

# 10

# On the Road Again

To fight and conquer in all our battles is
not supreme excellence. Supreme
excellence consists in breaking the
enemy's resistance without fighting.
—SUN TZU

When it comes to dealing with the law of
averages, it's best to be a habitual
offender.
—WALTER SLOVOTSKY

Jason had always had good teachers, he had long
ago decided. Valeran hadn't just made him a good
knifeman, a better swordsman, a decent rifleman
and pistolshot, but had taught him that there was
a time and place for the use of all weapons, except one.

*That one, boy, is your mind,* the grizzled old
warrior had said, more than once. *Never pays to
put that one away; always makes sense to keep it
well-oiled and active.*

Sometimes, though, it was too active.

He sipped at a tepid glass of water from the pitcher on the nightstand, then set it down and walked back to where, splashed with early morning sunlight, Ahira was packing their gear. Ahira's was, as always, packed neatly: each item of clothing carefully folded and laid in, compactly, but seemingly randomly, like how in an old-style stone fence, the stones no two alike, somehow were stacked so as to bring order from chaos.

Toryn's rucksack was simply a container of more sacks: thin canvas bags, some containing clothes, squeezed and wrapped in cord, others bulging with tools or bottles. Incongruously, a small painting of a seascape, perhaps twice the size of Jason's hand, lay on top of the pile. Toryn picked it up for a moment and smiled at it before wrapping it in an oilskin and stowing it away.

"I've saved you some room," he said.

It was all Jason could do not to see how badly this would all end as he finished stuffing a spare jerkin into Toryn's rucksack. It had been rolled tightly, then bound with string, making it as compact as was possible, and it was about the last thing that was going to go into Toryn's rucksack, whether or not it was the last thing they wanted to put into Toryn's rucksack.

Jason grunted as he strapped the cover flap over the mouth of the rucksack, then grunted again as he hoisted it to his shoulder.

Ahira shook his head. "No. It doesn't have to be easy, but it has to _look_ easy."

"I don't have your strength."

"So you'll just have to try harder to make it look like you're not trying harder, eh?" The dwarf walked over to the side of the room, where Jason's rucksack lay, one oversized bedroll strapped to its top, another to its bottom.

It wouldn't stand a close inspection, but it looked like the sort of oversized packs that dwarves typically carried; and large as the pack was, it didn't look large enough to contain the girl.

Which it didn't. Not all of her.

Ahira had cut the bottom and top out of his leather rucksack, and now Marnea was curled up painfully tightly inside the shell, kneeling sideways, a blanket wrapped and tied around her legs from knee to toe simulating the bedroll on the bottom, and her head concealed in the false bedroll on top—a wicker cylinder, open at the bottom, that had been a footstool when Jason had gone to sleep, but that Ahira's clever hands had unwoven, then rewoven.

It hadn't been possible for Jason and Toryn to stow Ahira's gear in their own rucksacks, but they'd supplemented them with a few of the spare sailcloth bags that Ahira had, and packed everything as tightly as they could.

"Everybody ready?" Ahira asked.

Jason nodded.

"Now all we have to do is wait for Toryn to get—"

The door swung open at that, and Toryn walked in, pulling a small pair of sandals from inside his tunic.

"Done, and rather brilliantly so," he said, tossing the sandals to Ahira, who stuffed them into the middle of one of the sailcloth bags. Toryn smiled. "Assuming this works, it should be good fun."

Jason stopped himself from saying something about how it wasn't fun, it was important, it was serious, because Toryn would just have laughed at him.

Ahira gave the bag a friendly pat. "Time to be silent," he said. "One grunt could give us away." She would be all but motionless anyway, what with the way her legs were tied into the blanket, and the blanket tied to the bottom of the rucksack. Her arms were jammed tightly against her chest in the main body of the bag, clothing stuffed in to break the bulges of her elbows, but that was about all.

If the confinement made her scream out or grunt, it would quickly be all over.

Toryn adjusted the hem of his tunic, and hefted at his swordbelt, before running fingers through his hair, messing it slightly. "Everybody ready?" he asked.

His moves were smooth and unconcerned, as though he had done this a thousand times before. Jason envied him that self-confidence. Jason was afraid that every twitch of his hand betrayed that he was up to something, that even a blind man could see, would see, that he was up to something, that his voice would crack.

There was a bitter bile taste at the back of his tongue, and for a moment, he thought he would throw up.

Jason forced himself to nod. "Ready," he said, willing his voice not to crack.

"Now, if you please," Ahira said.

Toryn strode to the door and flung it open. *"Where's the girl?"* he shouted, as he stepped out into the corridor, shouting as he went, Jason lagging behind him.

Mikyn's visit had apparently put things on a higher state of alert than Jason would have normally expected. There were shouts down the corridor, and within a few moments, two armsmen appeared, the senior rubbing sleep from his eyes with one hand while the other still fiddled with the buckle of his broad swordbelt, the junior one, maybe only a couple years older than Jason, fully awake, despite the hour.

"Some problem, Journeyman?" the senior armsman grunted. He had finally finished with his swordbelt, and was rubbing a thick hand against the stubble on his chin.

"There is rather more than some minor problem," Toryn said, with a sneer. "I woke early, and went for my dawn constitutional. When I came back, the girl Marnea was gone. Escaped."

"More likely to be about her duties, I'd presume," the armsman said, unimpressed. He jerked his chin at his junior. "Felken, go see if you can find her—start off with the slave quarters, and then check the kitchen. If you have to, see if his Lordship's guard—Olsett, no?—admitted her to his Lordship's quarters, but keep your voice down; I'll not want Lord Pelester wakened just because some slaver is upset because he missed a morning poke before going on his way."

Toryn's lips whitened. "If all of Lord Pelester's men are such idiots, it's a surprise that the Warrior didn't slaughter you all in your beds. Festen," he said, beckoning at Jason, "come with me—we have to see the Lord. Denerrin—saddle the horses, load our gear, and bring the horses along."

Jason didn't like the slaver, but he had to admire the calm assurance with which Toryn gave orders, never once glancing toward the rucksack containing Marnea.

Ahira shrugged, as he casually lifted that rucksack as though it weighed nothing. "Lend a hand, eh?" he asked the nearest of the armsmen. Jason had been against Ahira asking for that, but the dwarf said it would be out of character not to, and that not employing local help would mean leaving Marnea alone at one point or another.

"I thought dwarves were strong enough to carry for three."

"Five," Ahira said, tucking one of the sailcloth bags under his arm. "Problem is bulk, not weight." He looked at Jason. "Watch out for the boss."

Jason had to run to catch up with Toryn.

"It's my fault," Toryn said, not waiting to be asked before he poured himself a mug of the tea on Pelester's polished marble table under the crabapple tree. "And I can't tell you how angry it makes me," he said, his light tone giving the lie to his words.

The lord's private suite, through which they had been conducted, was large, light, and airy, light and air in the bedroom provided by the wide doors that opened on three sides of it, opening out into the atrium garden: the lord's sleeping chamber was a tongue, thrust into the garden, protected by the red brick walls of the residence. There were other openings in the walls, but they were only horizontally slitted windows, set just below the juncture of ceiling and floor. Lesser beings would be allowed to share the fresh breeze of the lord's private garden, and perhaps a distant scent of patchouli and sunbaked endester, but not the explosion of fiery red-orange sunblossoms that rimmed the garden, or the cool greens of the broadleaved trees.

"I understand why I am upset," Pelester said, not sounding at all upset, "but why are you so concerned?" Thick-fingered hands picked up a filigreed silver eating prong, speared a bacon-wrapped morsel of something white—fish, perhaps? or veal?—and popped it in his mouth. Unmindful of the early morning chill, he wore a thin satin dressing gown, its broad sleeves hemmed with silver thread in a design of rearing horses. To the left of his plate, a steaming mug of hot tea sat; to the right, a small silver bell lay on its side in an intricately carved wooden cradle. "It wouldn't seem to be your problem, but mine."

"If you don't ask yourself any questions, so it would," Toryn said.

"Questions?"

"Questions. Like: why should she try to escape now?" Toryn rested a hip on the table as he sipped at the tea, not apparently noticing Pelester's glare. "Just days after you've lent her to the Warrior? And then me? And the morning after I told her that I suspected she knew more than she was letting on."

"What made you suspect that?"

Toryn's grin was insultingly broad. "I didn't, but it seemed to be worth a try before I left her in Festen's hands. She overplayed the innocence, just a little, I finally decided. I'm almost but not quite sure she knew something, and I was going to spend the day questioning her. Her escaping proves that I was right."

He reached out and grabbed a fist-sized loaf of bread from a plate and tossed it to Jason, then picked up another and dipped it in a brown sauce from a tureen.

Pelester's mouth quirked into a frown, but then relaxed. "All it proves," Pelester said, "is that you scared her into doing something . . . foolish."

"It isn't foolish for her to try to escape if she makes good her escape."

"Please," Pelester said, raising a hand, "this is not something new. My family has been keeping slaves for generations. My slave-keeper has a lock of her hair and some nail clippings safely stored, and I've a fast pair of horses heading for Abereen and a wizard; I'll have a troop of men on her trail by tomorrow morning," Pelester said. "Would you care to accompany them?"

"No, I'd rather preempt them." Toryn shook his head. "I'd rather find her before then. Our horses are rested, but I'll want to move quickly—lend me three more and we should have her back and put to the question by tomorrow morning, instead of just starting to search then."

"And how do you expect to find her?"

Toryn nodded at Jason. "Festen here was born a woodsman near Wehnest—he can track a quarry anywhere, particularly if he's had a scent

of it." Toryn smiled. "And he's had more than that
of little Marnea." He considered it for a moment.
"She's fleeing on foot, likely staying off the
roads—likely we can pick up her trail quickly,
and ride her down by nightfall, and have her talking before your noble head rests on its pillow. I'll
bet gold-for-silver he can find her footprints before you can finish your breakfast."

Jason kept his smile inside. This was likely to
be true enough, given that Toryn had just been
out for a walk in Marnea's sandals, making those
footprints.

Pelester nodded. "Very well." He raised a cau-
tionary finger. "But I'm fond of the little chit—I
don't object to you passing her around among
yourselves this night, but I don't want her
brought back seriously damaged."

"I know my business," Toryn said. "A few
bruises and scratches are to be expected—"

"—and are acceptable. A girl so badly abused
that I have to send for the Hand, and then deal
with screams at night, is not." Pelester rubbed at
an earlobe.

Toryn bowed. "Of course."

"Then you shall have the extra horses, and my
best wishes, as well." Pelester reached for the silver bell.

Ahira had their horses saddled and loaded by the
time Jason and Toryn reached the stables, which

in Pemburne Keep was an old low stone building built up against the main wall, a slanted, lean-to-style shingle roof above it serving to keep out the weather.

As he entered through the broad doors, straw gently crunching under his feet, it was all Jason could do not to gag at the reek of rotting manure. Didn't they ever muck this place out? Not that it would do a lot of good, what with there being too little ventilation.

But it would be a start.

The rigged rucksack where Marnea was hidden had been strapped to the saddle of the largest of their horses, the bay gelding Jason had been riding, and Ahira was busily engaged in some discussion with the two armsmen.

He turned at Jason's and Toryn's approach, and just for a moment, the mask of the dour and phlegmatic dwarf dropped: his eyes went wide beneath his heavy brows, and his thick lips mouthed the words: _We have to hurry._

It took a moment for Jason to figure it out— the rucksack was twitching, and while that motion was momentarily being hidden by the bulk of the big gelding, all it would take for Marnea to be discovered would be one of the armsmen walking around the other side of the animal, or somebody else walking in. One sneeze, one cough, one sound could expose them all.

Toryn raised a palm. "Quickly, young Festen—

take the bay and go see if you can pick up the girl's trail. I'd try the woods to the north, but that's just a guess. Denerrin and I will follow, with the spare horses."

Jason nodded. "Yes, Journeyman." Careful not to touch the rucksack—he had the probably foolish fear that if he so much as brushed it with a finger, it would all fall apart, everything would all fall apart—he pulled himself up to the saddle and kicked the horse into a fast walk out through the broad doors and into the day, out of the stench of the stables.

The gate to the keep was open, and the guards clearly had no orders to stop him; one raised a hand in a cursory greeting and farewell as he rode through, careful to keep the horse at a brisk walk that had the rucksack constantly bouncing, albeit just a little.

It was hard to tell if Marnea was still moving, or why, and he didn't dare ask as he rode through the streets that were already busy. It was a market day, and rough tables were being set up to line Pemburne's broad main street, the street that led up to and technically into the keep itself.

He thought of asking somebody which way was the quickest way out of town, but it was better not to; he left via the guard station that had admitted them the day before, and then thought about the effect of a more rapid gait on poor Marnea in the rucksack before he decided that

he couldn't afford the consideration—not hurry-
ing would look funny—and kicked the horse into
a canter toward the woods to the north.

When he was sure that he was far enough
away that the wind couldn't carry his voice back
to the guards, he let some of the tension ease out
of his shoulders.

"You can relax now," he said.

There was a groan from the blanket on top of
the rucksack. "I thought I was going to throw up,"
Marnea said, her voice muffled. "The smell—I
kept gagging, and trying not to move, not to say
anything."

Jason repressed a shudder. That would have
been real, real bad. If they'd been caught at that
point, fighting their way out might have been
possible, but escaping from a quickly gathered
troop of Pelester's armsmen would not.

Now, with a little luck—not much, just a little
—they would be at least a day away before
Pelester had reason to even suspect that he had
been swindled, and little enough reason, at that.
Toryn and his companions were on Marnea's trail,
he would think, and if none of them were heard
from, why, what was so surprising about that? Despite Toryn's brags about Festen's abilities, Festen
had simply been unable to find the girl, and the
slaver and his two companions had simply continued on the path of the Warrior, or Mikyn, or whatever he called himself. The next time a Guild

slaver passed through, Pelester would present a bill for the horses, but the Guild's credit was still good.

Jason had to chuckle. There was something sweet about the Guild having to pay for horses that he and Ahira had stolen from a slave owner.

It was a Walter Slovotsky sort of thing to do, and he liked it. He wished for a moment he had a mirror handy—did his own smile announce how clever he was feeling?

"Don't worry," he said. "Another little while, and we'll be in the forest, and when the others join us, I'll let you out of there, and you can ride like a real person." They would dress her in a spare tunic and trousers of Jason's, and tie her hair back, sailor-style. From a distance, she would pass just fine, and there was no need to get close to anybody.

The path through the forest ran through an open meadow, where after a distant doe raised its head and fled in alarm, they were all alone.

Why wait?

Jason rode off the path into the grasses that were high enough to rub at his boots. He quickly dismounted, and lifted the rucksack-cum-Marnea down to the ground. A few quick strokes of his beltknife, and she was free, curled on her side, hidden in the grass.

He helped her to her feet. "If you hear anything, just lie down in the grasses, and don't say anything, don't move," he said. "I want to wait for Ahira and Toryn, and—" he saw how her eyes went wide.

Damn. She hadn't known that the dwarf was Ahira, and Jason had just told her. Not good. Ahira was every bit as famous as Walter Slovotsky. Letting his identity slip wasn't dangerous, probably, not as bad—or as good, if it all worked out—as Jason having revealed who he was, but just a bad policy. Don't tell people things they don't need to know, Valeran always used to say. It's no favor to trust somebody with a secret that won't do him any damn good.

He was already pulling clothes from his own rucksack, and she was already stripping off her thin gray shift, carelessly tossing it aside; he snatched it up and stuffed it in a pocket.

Naked in the golden sunlight, she was slim and lovely, but he was Jason Cullinane, dammit, not Walter Slovotsky, and he used his _mind_ for thinking. He helped her into a bulky tunic and a pair of trousers, belting it tightly at the hips—not her slim waist—with a leather strap before tying her hair back with a small thong.

From a distance, she would pass, but close-up, it was hopeless. The smooth complexion, naturally reddened at cheekbones and along the jawline, and the full lips weren't those of a boy, or a man.

She smiled, not at all shyly, and put her arms

around his neck, pulling herself close to him. "Thank you so much for getting me out of there," she said, lifting her face to be kissed.

She was gorgeous, and last night had been remarkable, but it occurred to Jason that perhaps Marnea wasn't overly bright. If somebody were to be riding through the forest, the last thing they ought to be seeing was two people kissing.

Hoofbeats sounded off in the distance; with a quick, hissed order to stay, he pushed her down in the tall grasses, and led his horse away, toward where tall, gnarled oaks stood at the edge of the meadow, as though the leafy giants had slowly, deliberately, over eons, waddled up to the meadow, only to stop at its shore.

But it was only Ahira and Toryn, the dwarf frowning as he bounced on the back of his small gray gelding, the slaver smiling ear-to-ear as he led a string of three horses, one of them, a brown mare, already saddled, the other two loaded with gear.

Jason called to Marnea, and led his own horse back up to the path, then helped her up to the saddle.

Toryn chuckled. "That was fun. I haven't had such a good time in years—even better than the time I got treble price for an old lame farmhand, I swear."

Jason normally would have been angered by the comparison, and he knew he should have been angered by the comparison, but things were going well, and he couldn't help returning Toryn's infectious smile for just a moment.

"Where to?" he asked, turning to Marnea.

She sat silently on the back of her horse for a moment. "Lesteen," she said, quietly. "He said he had some business in Lesteen, then he'd come back for me. He should be on his way now."

Ahira nodded. "Figure three days to Lesteen, one day scouting it out before he strikes, then another three days back to Pemburne. If he's told you the truth, if you're telling us the truth, we'll catch up with him sometime tomorrow, or the next day."

"Then let's be about it," Toryn said. "But I do foresee a problem, starting tomorrow. Pelester will have a wizard and a tracker on our trail—on Marnea's trail. Perhaps you'll want to reconsider—"

Jason was already reaching for the small amulet on the thong around his neck. He edged his horse over toward Marnea, then handed it to her. "Put this on." He turned back to Toryn. "Prevents being located with magic."

"You do have such wonderful tricks available, don't you?" Toryn's smile was condescending. "Well, then let's ride, shall we?"

They camped that night on a rocky outcropping high on a hillside. A cookfire would have been

asking for trouble, although from whom Jason
didn't know—so they didn't light one anyway, and
instead made a full dinner of fresh morning bread
and the thick garlicky sausages that Toryn had
demanded from Pelester's kitchen on his and
Ahira's way out, all washed down with a light,
sweet wine, chilled by wetting the wineskin and
hanging it in the cool night breeze. It tasted of
apples and flowers and was ever so lightly honeyed.

Jason took first watch, while the others curled
up in their blankets. He set his own blanket on a
fairly flat rock and set his weapons down beside
him. A small gathering of houses lay far down the
hill; he could see an occasional spark from a
chimney, and a drifting wind brought the wood-
smoke to his nose. And far beyond that, the rocky
coast broke on the Cirric, the water black and
glossy under the blinking of the stars and the
slow, pulsating throb of the distant faerie lights.

They could have had it right, or they could
have had it wrong. But they were close to Mikyn
right now. There were two roads that led from
Pemburne to Lesteen; one, a broad highway,
skirted the lowland towns, while the other wound
its way up through the rocky, wooded hills, then
back down. The two joined—well, the smaller
one joined the larger one at a tiny village called
Ekenden, an old Dwarvish word meaning, literally, "Nothing." Jason figured they would reach

Ekenden the next day, if they pushed themselves
and their horses hard enough.

And then . . .

And then it would be over, one way or the
other.

Too many faerie lights tonight, most of them
strung out near the horizon in a ragged line that
pulsated in a slow, even rhythm through a series
of dark blues and blood reds, punctuated only occasionally by a throb of green or a flash of yellow.

No, not too many. More than he was used to,
he thought, but that didn't mean that there were
too many. The rift between Faerie and reality had
been healed; he had been there to help, and of all
the things that had come of that, more faerie
lights weren't a real problem.

He looked over to where Marnea slept, huddled in her blankets, the first night she had slept
free in half a dozen years. This counted for more,
he decided, or at least as much. He wasn't ready
to deal with big issues, just one at a time.

Which was probably how Mikyn saw it. But
give it a few more days—they would bring Mikyn
in, and end some of it. Let Toryn report that Karl
Cullinane was dead and that the Warrior was just
another Home raider, one who had gone too far
and been reined in. Let the Guild argue, for the
length and breadth of the Eren Regions, that this
suggested that the Home raiders were too violent,
too crazy to be trusted.

They were winning, a little bit at a time.

There was a sound behind him. He had expected Marnea, but to his surprise it was Toryn, wearing only a pair of trousers, his feet and chest bare, no weapon in sight.

"It's not your watch yet," Jason said. By now, he trusted Toryn enough to believe that the slaver would keep a good watch, but that didn't mean he was eager to demonstrate that. *Trust* wasn't a word that went well with *slaver*.

Toryn shrugged as he sat down beside Jason, looking down toward the lowlands. "I'm not sleepy," he said. "I would guess I caught enough last night, while you were otherwise occupied. How was she?" He held up a palm. "Apologies, young Cullinane, genuine apologies. I just meant to make polite conversation." He chuckled thinly. "I would take it you get many such . . . gestures of appreciation in your trade."

"It's been known to happen," Jason said, trying to sound older and more experienced than he was, fairly sure it had come off okay, but no better than that.

Toryn chuckled thinly. "Then I guess I should inform the Guild that we should only travel with ugly slaves, of ill temper and little skill in the blankets, eh? So that, at least, while you're celebrating our deaths, instead of having some lovely's heels drumming a mad tattoo on your hairy backside, you will be fending off the attentions and affections of some pig-snouted Sireene, her breath reeking of garlic."

Jason couldn't help smiling. "Yeah, that would do, at that."

Toryn clapped him on the shoulder. "To tell you the truth, young Cullinane, when this is all over, I'll miss you. You have such a simple way about you. Mind, once I'm back in Pandathaway and the geas is removed, I'd happily slit your throat—but even then, I'd miss you."

"Particularly then, Toryn. I wouldn't be a good audience if I was dead, and you like having an audience for your . . . wit."

"I'd say you wound me, if you were capable of it—or if it wasn't true, Jason." Toryn's smile was warm in the darkness, and for a moment, Jason thought he was going to say something else, something important, but then he just asked, "Are you literate in Erendra, or just that Englits of yours?"

"English," Jason said. "And yes. I can make my way through the Erendra glyphs, and even the low form of the Moderate People's runes. Why?"

Toryn shrugged. "Nothing of import. I thought I might like to write you a letter, after all this is over, although I'm not sure who I would entrust with it, or who you wouldn't kill." He chuckled. "Go to sleep, Jason. I'd like to be alone with my geas and my thoughts."

# 11

## Pandathaway

Nine-tenths of wisdom consists in being
wise in time.

—THEODORE ROOSEVELT

Serendipity isn't just when you're
overrewarded for reasonable effort, like
when you dig for worms and strike gold.
It's also when you're cleaning your gun,
and you've stupidly forgotten to unload
it, and it goes off unexpectedly, hitting
the burglar you didn't see square between
the eyes.

—WALTER SLOVOTSKY

There're two ways to pick up a trail, and the
easier one, I'd decided, was to do it via finding
hunters, not prey.

Nobody had any more interest in where Mikyn
was than the Slavers Guild, and it would likely be
easier to pick up Jason's and Ahira's trail by finding Mikyn's.

All of which suggested to me, clever fellow
that I am, that the best way to find the kid and
the dwarf was to get the Guild to tell me.

"And how are you going to do that, Walter Slovotsky?" Bren Adahan asked, raising his voice only enough to carry over the rush of the wind, no more. Too careful, but the baron was always too careful—at, by my guess, five thousand feet in the air above a rocky, wave-beaten shoreline, we were unlikely to be overheard, and equally unlikely to be spotted, save as a shadow against the star-spattered sky that would be more likely to be thought a cloud than a dragon with seven men strapped to his back.

Below us, Pandathaway was spread out across the shoreline, like, well, a city spread out across a shoreline: bounded by waters that seemed oily in the starlight, most of the city dark, save for elf-lights at the junctures of major roads and for the lanterns of patroling wardens. I let my eye follow the Street of the Wheelwrights to where it met the Avenue of Elms, and found the Great Library, although I needn't have gone to quite so much trouble. The whole building was sparking gently, like a Van de Graaff generator; some wizard was doing something there, and that was presumably a side effect.

While the constant beat of Ellegon's huge wings didn't change, I felt us climbing for a moment, and then suddenly falling. I'm sure I would have fallen from my place if I hadn't been strapped in—or if I hadn't been clinging desperately to Ellegon's rigging.

*What was that?*

\*There's a fire smoldering in the cesspit—my old, err, place of employment.\* For just a moment I caught a flash of how Ellegon had hated being chained for centuries in that cesspit, forced to flame the wastes of Pandathaway's sewers into fog and ash, every moment a stinking agony, and how sweet the first few breaths of free air had tasted in his nostrils, but it was only for a moment.

When the dragon spoke again, his mental voice was calm and level. \*We caught a thermal for a moment, then lost it. Not to worry; I'll get you at least most of the way to the ground in one piece.\*

As a skydiver friend of mine used to say, it's only the last inch that hurts.

\*Yeah, but it hurts a *lot*.\*

The city fell behind us, and Ellegon pulled my heart to my mouth by standing himself on a wing as he circled down in a too-tight spiral that at least pressed me toward his back, not away from it, but which also pulled groans and cries from everybody except Bren Adahan—

—well, and me. I wasn't about to show weakness while the baron was showing strength.

A couple of miles to the west of the city a small hill thrust out above the rest of the rocky shoreline, rimmed by a beard of gnarled old elms that had never quite managed to ensconce themselves on its rocky top. Scallen's Anvil, it was called, after a famous smith, and during the autumn thunderstorms, while wizards' spells warded the lightning away from the city, people would watch the lightning bolts strike the anvil over and over again . . .

The rocky surface was cracked and cratered in spots, but it was shielded from direct view by the trees.

Ellegon landed lightly, claws scrabbling for a moment on the rock while his wings continued to beat hard, as though he could leap into the air and avoid a dragonbaned arrow.

As maybe he could.

*Grab your baggage and jump,* he said, settling down onto the rock. *This train does not stop at this station.*

There are advantages to dealing with a team that's worked together before; by the time Bren Adahan and I had retrieved our own gear and climbed down over Ellegon's scaly sides, the five of them had gotten not only themselves unhooked and down, but all their gear as well. One of them checked over the packs while two others gave a quick once-over to the network of harness that had kept us and our gear on his back, tightening a buckle here and there. If it started to slip off during flight, Ellegon would have no choice but to claw it away, rather than risk having it tangle him up when he landed.

*Two days,* he said, leaping into the air, the wind from his fast-moving wings threatening to blow me over toward the trees. If two of the trackers hadn't already been sprawled out over the bags, the luggage would have been blown away. *I will check back in two days, and again in five. After that, you are on your own.*

After a few years doing this, some of the routine had become automatic. Henden, Darren, and Lerdeen had already stolen off into the trees, trying to see if there was anybody waiting for us out there, while Chit and Darnelen each produced a brace of pistols and sought cover at the edge of the treeline.

But after a few minutes passed, there was no sound save for the whistling of the wind through the trees, the distant, muted crashing of the waves against the shoreline far below, and a three-part whistle of a swamp-lark that was echoed by Chit, while Darnelen nodded to Bren Adahan and me that it was safe to proceed.

Before the sun fully rose above the Cirric, we had made it to the gates of Pandathaway; by noon, we were safely settled into a suite of rooms at an inn near the shore, and with Chit and Henden on watch, I was fully asleep.

The daytime is for honest men; I'm a night person.

Turning a landbound noble into a sailor is either a trivial matter or an impossible one. Middle Lands noblemen tend to wear their hair long in the back, so tying it back in a sailor's ponytail was easy, although they don't wear it long enough for a full sailor's braid. The calluses a sailor gets from hauling ropes are similar enough to those a lord can get working the fields, and some people just callus more easily than others, anyway.

That part was easy.

"So, why," Bren Adahan asked, as I snipped away at his beard—with an idle thought as to what else of his I'd like to snip, given the chance—to round out the squareness of it and make it look less well tended, "do we have to be sailors, anyway?"

Three of the trackers were asleep in the corner of the room, their weapons close to hand, while Chit and Darnelen took first watch. Which mainly consisted of playing a game of bones over a pot of hot tea, although they had set up their table in the middle of the deep rug, their chairs positioned kitty-corner, so that Chit was facing the doors to the balcony while Darnelen faced the door that led out into the hall and downstairs. It's best to work with people you know, trust, and like, but working with competent professionals isn't a bad second choice.

I sighed. "For one thing, because sailors talk. They drink, they sing, and they talk. Aboard ship, there's either a lot that needs to be done right now—say, when you're changing sails—or there's next to nothing, and all you can do is talk. Not always truthfully, mind, but there's a fine line between being known for exaggerating along the edges of a story—which only tends to improve your reputation as a storyteller—and being an out-and-out liar." I gestured at him to stand up. "Now try walking again."

The last thing I really wanted was a partner on this, but . . .

I shook my head. "You're walking like a Middle Lands nobleman," I said in a low voice, barely above a whisper, drawing a grin from Darnelen, which drew a glare from Adahan.

"I *am* a Middle Lands nobleman," Adahan said.

"Why don't you fucking say it a little louder, asshole?" I asked.

Darnelen's smile broadened as he picked up the cup and lightly shook it, then dumped the tiny bones out on the playing board. "I pick this, and this, leaving . . . a Minor Triumph," he said, moving a copper coin to the betting square. "Your throw."

"Try again," I said to Adahan. If Adahan couldn't pick up the walk, I could leave him in the rooms with the trackers, and go out by myself.

And he couldn't. A landbound man expects the ground underneath him to be stable; he carries his weight on the flat of his feet and sometimes on his heels, his knees often locked, sometimes off-balance, because what does it matter? The ground underneath his feet is solid as, well, the ground.

A sailor can't afford to do that. He supports his weight on the balls of his feet, knowing that any time he locks his joints in place they can become a lever to knock him off his feet, and maybe over the railing. The deck underneath his feet is always shifting, and while he can usually anticipate the way it will shift, he's going to be wrong every now and then, when a wave is larger than expected or a sudden gust of wind fills the sails or a change in wind empties them.

So he's always in balance, but ready to catch hold of something if knocked off-balance—

—sort of like a thief, really. And not a bad way to run your life when you think of it.

And Bren just didn't have it.

I shook my head. "Sorry, Baron. You won't pass; I'll have to do it alone."

He thought it over for a moment, then nodded. "Very well, Walter Slovotsky. As we decided, you are in charge, and I'll not endanger you with my incompetence," he said, the tightness of his mouth giving the lie to his quiet words.

I threw on a cloak, hefted my seabag and headed downstairs, passing through the common room without drawing any comment about the sailor who had come out of the room that seven soldiers had walked into. If you sling it sailor-fashion over your shoulder, it's a seabag; if you tuck it awkwardly under your arm, it's just a bag. We weren't carrying ourselves as sailors; we were, officially, seven unemployed soldiers looking for work, perhaps as a wizard's bodyguard, perhaps as guards on a caravan of some sort.

Nothing unusual about that in Pandathaway, which was still the most important trading center in the Eren regions. Hell, you could even buy Home wootz in the Metalworkers' district.

The common room was almost empty, although not for any reason I could see. Over by the man-high fireplace, two hulking men, each sporting a variety of scars and missing parts, were involved in a drinking competition, while next to the beaded curtain leading to the kitchens, Orvin the innkeeper, who was built more like a stevedore than anything else, kept a distant skeptical watch. My guess was that the bout would end in some sort of fight, and so was his, although it probably wouldn't be a serious fight.

But it wasn't my fight. With a brief nod to Orvin, I walked out into the night.

The Tavern of the Rusty Ox—I'm sure that there was a story behind the name, but I never did get the chance to ask—was on Old Horse Street, just south of the broad plaza where Old Horse intersects with Horse Street and with New Horse Street. (Sometime, just give me five minutes alone with a ball peen hammer and the idiot who laid out Pandathaway. Five minutes, that's all I ask.) In the center of the plaza was a double-lifesized statue of, unsurprisingly, a horse—and a nice one at that—from the long face and high head, Pandathaway-bred. It looked all glossy in the dark, lit only by the stars above and the six elf-lights perched high on poles ringing the plaza.

Which didn't leave much shadow. I like shadow; it hides me well.

So instead of hiding near the statue, I found a spot under the eaves of a dark, unlit building, and huddled down in my cloak. There wasn't much traffic this late at night, on foot or on horse or wheel, as most businesses were long since closed up and most Pandathaway residents off to bed, while most of those businesses catering to the late-night crowd, be they taverns or brothels, were down by the water.

I didn't have long to wait until a cloaked figure, the seabag slung properly over his shoulder giving a lie to his landlubber's gait, walked out of Old Horse Street.

I reached out a hand and tapped him on the

shoulder, rewarded by a flash of panic on his face as he spun around, one hand going for the hilt of the sailor's knife he carried at his belt.

"Good evening," I said. "If you insist on coming along, we'll just put a pebble in your boot, and let you be a limping sailor. Just keep your mouth shut, and let me do the talking, eh?"

"Why didn't you mention that before?"

*Because I don't really want you along, but I'd rather have you along with me than out mucking about by yourself and maybe getting us all in trouble,* I thought. "Didn't think of it," I said.

He looked smug. "I thought so."

Face flushed with bitter beer, Oren of the *Orumeé* leaned back and took another long pull at his pewter tankard. "Been close to a year since I've seen you, Wen'l," he said, wiping the foam from his lips with the back of his arm. "What ships you been working of late?" Think thick: thick fingers, nails short-bitten, gripping the tankard; thick, barrel-chested body; thick black beard, more hacked into shape than trimmed; thick lips; thick voice because too much drinking had made his tongue thick. Thick.

"None, for the past while." I shrugged. "Tried a hand at living ashore," I said, and went into a long and somewhat improbable story about a young wanton whose father owned a winery. I had to move the events around; it had happened a few years back and a few countries away, but that's often the way things are when you're telling a story that has the liability of being true.

"Didn't take, eh?" he asked.

I shrugged. "You know how it is. Once you get used to the feel of sliding lines burning blisters on your palms, of cold food twice a day and warm ale once, of splinters in your feet and rain in your face . . ."

He laughed. "Of a sudden roll slapping the port railing against your kidney, of sleeping in a cramped hold with a dozen unbathed sailors, of surly captains and low pay . . . ah, how could you ever give up such a life?"

"I tried, give me that."

"But it called you back."

"It always does," I said. I sipped at my own beer. I had the distinct impression that the brewer had let some of the hops pass through the digestive tract of a goat before roasting, but you can't have everything. It was cold and wet, and I was thirsty and dry.

Bren Adahan was glaring at me.

"Your friend doesn't talk much," Oren said.

"He's a mute," I said. "Made the mistake of making fun of an island witch, out Filikos way. She made his tongue go stiff, and his pecker limp," I said, I guess turning one of my own wishes into a story for the third time that night, much to Bren's discomfiture.

Rattling off another improbable tale while listening with one ear came easy. Over in the corner, two sailmakers were haggling with the captain of the *Busted Jaw* over the cost of a new balloon sail, while farther down the long, rough table where we sat, a trio of seamen from a ship whose name I didn't catch were involved in a long discussion of the sanitary habits, such as they were, of the mate. Farther on down was a talk about what I took to be local politics, definitely involving entry fees and tariffs, while behind us a steersman from the *Teesia* was engaged in a stroke-by-stroke description of how he had spent his earnings across the street.

Nothing about the Warrior, and I wasn't going to be the one to bring it up.

One easy recipe to get into trouble: plop myself down in a tavern or in the drinking room of a bordello, and ask what the Slaver's Guild was up to, whether the Warrior had struck recently, and where. Repeat until somebody noticed that this Wen'l of Lundescarne (there really was a Wen'l of Lundescarne, but he was a peasant, and unlikely to be known beyond the Lundeyll markets, or anywhere more than five miles away from his cottage) seemed overly interested in the Warrior.

It would be simple.

It would be somewhat less simple to explain myself to the Guild Council proctors who were the Pandathaway police force, a group of serious unsmiling young men, handy with truncheon, knife, and sword, any of whom would be more than happy to trade in the head of Walter Slovotsky for an embarrassingly large amount of gold.

So I listened as much as I could and talked just enough to get a reputation as a brilliant raconteur, and drank half a mug of beer for every beer-and-refill I ordered.

It was the fifth place that I heard something.

". . . Pemburne, it was, that the Warrior last struck," a harsh voice somewhere behind me said. "Just days ago—we had to hold at Endeport while the local lord put some questions to some of our new hands, wondering if they might be him, traveling in disguise. You should have seen the way they surrounded us: two horsemen on the pier, bowmen behind them, a skiff-full of armsmen coming up on the starboard side, ready to board if we were to make a move. And then they took them off to see if—"

"They weren't him," a bored voice said, "or that would be the story. Get to the *story*, man."

To my right, Bren Adahan had stiffened, but I didn't think our companion across the table noticed, or noticed me kicking him under the table, gently enough not to draw a sound out of him, hard enough to make the point that he shouldn't seem to be particularly interested in this.

"Just his usual," the voice went on. "Although this time it was the lord's slave-keeper he killed, and he did it in the guise of a Guild Slaver. Seems a wizard turned him into the likeness thereof—"

"Oh? And what does a Guild Slaver look like? Or do you mean a specific one?"

"Who's telling the story? You or me? The lord was thinking of selling off some of his women-slaves, and turned the Warrior—thinking he's a Guild Slaver, mind—loose in their quarters for the night. Come morning, all twenty of the women were smiling, the slave-keeper was dead, drained of every drop of blood, his dead eyes and mouth wide, and the Warrior gone. I heard that he had turned himself into a raven and flew away, but that sounds unlikely." As though the rest of it sounded likely.

Bren's eyes caught mine, but I didn't nod.

Pemburne, eh? I needed a map, but that would have to wait for tomorrow. Tomorrow night, late tomorrow night, we'd be in the air. Ellegon would be able to pinpoint Jason's location, once we got close enough.

*Hang on, guys; I'll be there.* "I think I'll have another beer."

# 12

## Mikyn

It is not the critic who counts; not the
man who points out how the strong man
stumbles, or where the doer of deeds
could have done them better. The
credit belongs to the man who is actually
in the arena, whose face is marred by
dust and sweat and blood.
—THEODORE ROOSEVELT

Monkeys, whether you watch them in an
Other Side zoo or in a Salket forest, fight
the same way every time: they start off
by threatening, then escalate to pushing
and shoving, and then finally get down to
it. This may be a good idea for monkeys,
but it's a bad idea for humans. If you
learn to go from utter peace to all-out
war in a heartbeat, your chances of
survival go way up. Unless, of course, you
pick the wrong heartbeat in which to
go from peace to war, but there you
have it: the right policy doesn't do you
any good in the wrong situation.
—WALTER SLOVOTSKY

Ahira raised his left hand, then extended his thick index finger. *Single horseman ahead,* he sighed. "You'll hear him in a few minutes," he whispered.

The dwarf pulled on the reins—too gently, then too hard; Ahira never quite had gotten the hang of horses—slowing his gray gelding from a sullen walk to a sullen stop on the broad, flat road.

Jason was already out of his saddle.

The road twisted along a hillside underneath broadleaved trees. Flat enough to engineer with; even where it narrowed it was wide enough for two broad carts to pass each other, albeit carefully. Flat enough for four horses to ride abreast —although that would have put the outermost rider frighteningly close to the edge. And while the wooded hills behind them were overgrown with leafy beds of fern and ivy that twisted snakelike around the bases of the huge trees, here it was not overgrown at all, as though some wizard had cast a death spell on plants that would dare to try to invade the trees' domain.

Which was not particularly unlikely, come to think of it.

It was the third time this morning that Ahira had stopped all of them, and the third time this morning that Jason and Toryn had, at that command, quickly dismounted, and moved their saddles and bridles from their present mounts to rested ones, and the third time that Jason had managed to beat Toryn back into the saddle. Jason had had good teachers, and hadn't just spent more time on horseback than Toryn had; when the riding lesson ended, it was Jason who had unsaddled and rubbed down the animal, then watered and fed it, while Toryn had probably just handed his horse over to some slave to take care of.

So it was easily a minute before Toryn could possibly finish that Jason gripped the reins of the large roan gelding, put his foot into the stirrup, and hefted himself up to the saddle, kicking the horse into a slow canter, leaving the rest of them behind. If this horseman turned out to be a message courier from Estene, his leather shoulderbag bulging with correspondence, the way it had been the first time, or a squat Aersnter whose business on the road was not apparent, the way it had been the second time, it would be simple.

Jason would, for the third time this morning, slow his horse to a walk, because approaching a stranger quickly was a threat, and for the third time this morning hold up his right palm in a universal greeting that completely uncoincidentally demonstrated that he wasn't holding a weapon, and would accept the stranger's greeting with the same nod, and then simply wait beyond the next bend of the road and let the rest of them catch up to him. The dust his horse had kicked up would help to explain why the third member of Ahira's and Toryn's party coughed into a broad handkerchief that covered "his" face.

Jason was so ready for it to be another false alarm that there was a quick heartbeat where he didn't recognize Mikyn.

He could have argued that his old friend's thin brown beard had lightened marginally and thickened considerably since they'd last seen each other, and it certainly was true that Mikyn hadn't been nearly as battered looking in the old days, but mainly it was his eyes. They had always been Mikyn's eyes, nothing special or remarkable about them. Perhaps when Mikyn smiled, there used to be a certain something about the way they crinkled at the corners, or maybe there was something particular about the way he neither stared at nor looked away from things.

These eyes, sunken, stared out at him, holding his own without blinking, without any trace of kindness or hostility. He was Jason's age, and he had always looked older, but now he looked easily forty years old.

And there was something in his eyes. Something of determination at best, perhaps, but probably madness.

And then there was something in Mikyn's face, a flash of fear before the recognition set in, and then the suspicion.

"Jason," he said, and his face broke into a grin.

_Yes._

They had been searching for Mikyn, but Jason hadn't worked out even in his own mind what he would say. It all depended on which Mikyn they found—the boy who Jason used to go swimming with at Home, the friend who was found as often in the kitchen of the Old House as in his adopted family's house, the comrade-at-arms who Jason had once let down . . .

Or the cold-blooded killer who had all of the Middle Lands up in arms.

"Damn it, Mikyn," Jason finally said. "You're a hard man to find."

The grin broadened, but the stare was the same. "I meant it to be that way." A frown. "You're looking for me?"

"Yes. Time to come in. To lay it down for a while." _To have a bunch of folks who you might listen to explain to you that while the time may come to free slaves right and left, killing anybody in the way, the time isn't now, and isn't likely to come in our lifetimes._

"No. I still haven't found him, not yet. I figure that when I make enough trouble for them, they'll send him after me." He grinned wolfishly. "And until then, I free a few, I kill a few slave-owners."

_Him._ The slaver they'd met in Enkiar, the one who Mikyn was sure was the one that had abused him and his family, even though it was impossible, and Mikyn's plan madness even if it wasn't.

"I'm sure that'll bother them," Jason said. "Slitting their throats while they sleep. Hell, it bothers me."

A long pause. "It's easier that way. Nobody has the right to own anybody."

"Not arguing that," Jason said. "I'm arguing tactics—and I'm arguing—"

The slow clackity-clack of hoofbeats sounded off in the distance; Mikyn reached inside his cloak.

"Ta havath, eh?" Jason said. *Take it easy, huh?* "It's just the rest of them."

Mikyn's smile broadened when he saw Ahira, and even more a moment later. "Marnea," he said. "Well, I guess that saves me some trouble, eh?" He lifted his head. "Long time, Ahira."

Ahira clumsily reined in his horse, his head cocked to one side. "I wasn't sure you'd be back for her. Didn't sound like you," he said, dropping heavily from his saddle to the road. The dwarf stretched his broad shoulders, and rubbed idly at his backbone.

Mikyn snickered. "Just because I'm doing things my way instead of yours?"

"Something like that."

"Up yours." He shrugged. "You haven't introduced me to your friend."

A chill washed across Jason's back. What

would Mikyn do? What would Toryn do? He tried
to remember the exact words of the geas—

"Toryn, I want you to meet my friend and companion, Mikyn."

Mikyn looked at him strangely, but Jason
wasn't about to explain that Toryn's geas applied
to Jason and his companions, and he had to get
Mikyn under the tent of that promise right now.

Toryn smiled. "Toryn the Journeyman, they call
me."

"Ah." Mikyn nodded. "Journeyman engineer,
eh? They make them quicker every day. How is
_he_?"

Toryn shrugged. "Getting a little older every
year. Still sharp as always."

"That is the way of it."

"And you? How do you like this new career of
being the Warrior?" Toryn asked, his voice just
too calm, too level.

Mikyn smiled. "I like it well enough. Jason's
trying to talk me into giving it up for a while, with
some nonsense about how I can come home and
all will be forgiven, and—"

"I don't know why he'd want to do that," Toryn
said, with a quick smile. "When I'm here."

Mikyn shook his head, not understanding.

"You see," he said, "I'm not just Jason's associate—I'm a Journeyman—"

—_of the Slaver's Guild_, Jason completed in his
mind. _Of course._

He had been one step too slow, and Ahira with him. Toryn's geas prevented the slaver from attacking any of them—unless and until one of them attacked him. It did not prevent him from telling Mikyn that he was a Journeyman of—

"—of the Slaver's Guild, partnered with Jason and Ahira with their agreement."

Ahira was already moving, his feet pounding on the ground with a *thump-thump-thump* that sounded too slow, too late to be any good.

He reached Mikyn's side just as Mikyn's sword was clearing its scabbard. A short leap, a squat, and the dwarf launched himself into the air, knocking Mikyn from the back of his horse.

Jason eased himself out of the saddle. Mikyn was no match for Ahira's dwarven strength.

Toryn's hands had never come near the hilt of his own sword as Jason stalked toward him. "You had your warning, young Cullinane, from the dwarf," he said, ignoring the grunting and groaning. "As much fun as it's been to travel with you, you didn't expect me to not follow my orders, did you?" He held out his hands palms up. "Even if I hadn't wanted to, I was under geas for that, too, although one cast by a wizard of rather smaller stature than Vair the Uncertain. Voluntarily undertaken, you understand; the Guildmaster was afraid that I would find your companionship too agreeable, knowing what a sociable fellow I am."

Marnea was looking daggers at his back, and it

was all Jason could do not to draw his own sword. Toryn was probably as good with a blade as his swagger suggested, but Jason wasn't unfamiliar with it himself.

*"You will stay where you are,"* a harsh voice cried out.

Hoofbeats sounded from beyond the bend, a rapid pounding that slowed as the horses—Jason was sure it was at least six, maybe seven—came nearer.

Jason turned, toward where Ahira and Mikyn were still wrestling on the ground. Beyond them, sealing off any escape that way, three bowmen stood, arrows nocked, a fourth man holding their horses.

Lord Pelester, mounted on a huge white gelding, rode around the bend, trailed by a troop of half a dozen mounted soldiers, two with long lances pointed at Jason and the others, four with longswords naked in their hands.

"I was fooled once by a supposed slaver, Journeyman Toryn," he said. "I resolved not to be twice so fooled," he said. "You will all put up your weapons and surrender, or you will die where you are."

He was a young boy again, sitting in front of a campfire, listening to old Valeran hold forth. Not that it was any hardship to listen to his teacher talk endlessly, the voice hoarse from too many years of shouting commands to his troop.

"The thing of it is," the grizzled old warrior said, "that you always want to hold a little back. It's like keeping a reserve in battle: if it all goes to shit—and boy, more often than you'd like, it all goes to shit—you need something extra, to get you out.

"So you don't go all-out, because when you do that, you're going to fall down out of breath when it's all done, leaving yourself vulnerable. And you can't count on it being done in a few moments.

"So be careful, and don't go all-out. Unless . . ."

Jason had first learned not to walk into a line like that, and then, when he was older, not to leave a line like that hanging. "Unless?"

"Unless it's right. Then from flat-footed idleness you go into all-out action, without a breath, without a blink."

Without a blink, without a breath, Jason dove for the trees, drawing his sword as he did. Bowstrings thrummed.

# 13

## Ambush

The mice which helplessly find themselves between the cats' teeth acquire no merit from their enforced sacrifice.

—MAHATMA GANDHI

God, give me the strength to change that which can be changed, the strength to change that which probably can't be changed, and the strength to change that which can't possibly be changed. Hey, if You can't work miracles, what the hell good are You?

—WALTER SLOVOTSKY

They jumped us just outside the Inn of the Spotted Dog. I had about five seconds' warning.

You do this long enough, and if you survive, you develop nerve endings far beyond the envelope of your skin. It's not paranormal, although I can't always say what it is, and it's never, ever an excuse for not paying attention to your surroundings. Dead men don't pay attention to their surroundings.

I'd missed it.

Looking back, there had been something in the way a pair of burly, stocky men that I had mentally tagged as stevedores had looked at me, then looked away from my eyes. Looking back, maybe I caught a half nod or a partial silence from the group of men by the door who had moved just a little too much on their rough benches as Bren and I passed outside, or maybe I noticed the heavy way a cloak hung over the shoulder of another.

The night was clear and star-filled, good for flying. Give us another couple of hours, and we would be. First, we'd make our way to Scallen's Anvil just around midnight, and wait for the dragon. A few hours in the air, and we'd be at Pemburne. Hole up for the day, and then have Ellegon fly a spiral search pattern the next night, looking for Jason. Not a tight spiral, either: Ellegon had been mindtalking with Jason since before the boy was born, and could hear him further away than anybody else—even including Karl, when he was alive.

Then locate Mikyn, finish things up with him, and get Jason and Ahira home. Things would have to be straightened out with Thomen, but that could still be done, particularly with the influence of Barons Cullinane and Adahan—and Ellegon, for that matter.

It was going to be easy.

Until I heard an almost inaudible whisper behind me, and Bren Adahan leaned over and whispered one word: "Trouble."

I caught Adahan's arm and pulled him off-balance. "Hey, watch it," I said, loudly, maybe too loudly. "If you stumble and break your leg, I'll have to leave you behind." As he bumped against me, I muttered, "Break right: I'll break left," and moved, fast, to my left, not waiting for any acknowledgment.

I mean, if he wasn't any use in a fight, fuck him.

Something plucked at my right sleeve and something else tore at the right side of my face as I moved, running broken-field style. Back in the old days, it'd been my job to anticipate the sudden breaks in stride of somebody running with the ball so I could grab him and slam him to the ground, and even years later it gave me a sense of how not to be regular, predictable.

Seven broken steps took me to the mouth of an alley, and I ducked down and in and into shadow.

Given a large enough group, there's always going to be a hero, somebody brave and boldhearted enough to go in first. I had my sword out and ready, and sliced the tip past his swordpoint and through his neck, beating his sword aside and kicking him in the thigh as he staggered past, burbling until he crashed headfirst into a wall and fell down.

By that time, I was supposed to have myself set up, ready to take on the next one, which would make me a sucker for a two-man combination—one ready to knock my sword aside, another prepared to lunge past the first man and into me—so I was already halfway up the wall, my sword clamped in my teeth, supporting myself with my fingertips and toes against the tiny projections of the beams beyond the wattle-and-daub walls.

They surprised me: the first spun his cloak, the weights in the hem causing it to spread out nicely, and then they both lunged in underneath my feet.

I would have applauded, but that would have ruined the effect.

A throwing knife down the back of one neck slowed the first, and I landed both heels solidly on the shoulders of the other. His collarbone snapped like a piece of chalk, and he crumpled underneath me.

By then, of course, I had my sword back in my hand, and had probed delicately for the heart of the first man. The way to a man's heart is through his back, if possible, blade parallel to the ribs.

The other one was still moving, so I stepped on his sword hand while I slipped the tip of my blade in between his third and fourth ribs a couple of times until he quieted down.

I stood there for a moment, panting.

*Shit, I'm getting old.*

Ten years before, I could have done this without breaking a sweat.

Ten years before, I probably would have spotted the slip that Bren had made that had given us away—assuming it was Bren and not me who had fucked up.

Ten years before, I would have *known* it wasn't me that had screwed up, not merely doubted it.

Ten years before, I would have heard the men arranging themselves at the head of the alley long before their leader cleared his throat.

"Put up your sword, Walter Slovotsky," he said. "I have a rifle," he said redundantly, bringing his piece up and into line. "It's all over. Your friends back at the Inn are dead, and another squad should have your companion down by now."

There were three of them, blocking the entrance. I could have turned and run, but I was out of breath and they'd just run me down, even assuming that the one with the slaver rifle didn't miss. Even if I jumped aside fast enough to avoid his shot, I'd be off-balance, and they'd be on me before I could recover.

Ten years before, I might have been able to run out of this trap, but ten years before, I wouldn't have been in this trap.

But ten years before, I didn't have a snubnose revolver in a holster above my right buttock.

I lunged to one side as I drew it, and his rifle

went off with the loud and strangely flashless
*bang* of slaver rifles, wind whistling by my ear,
but as I lost my balance I was still able to get the
pistol up at the end of an outstretched hand.

I pulled the trigger, and flame spat out, rewarded by a scream and a groan.

They had been well-trained, for their time. A
flintlock pistol only held one round, and a fired
pistol was useless—the best technique was to
rush the pistoleer before he could bring another
pistol into play.

But technology had passed them by, and that
saved my life.

They rushed, and I shot four times more.

And then it was awfully quiet, what with the
bodies scattered around the alley. It would take
some time for the locals to investigate; being too
quick to go out and involve oneself with a fight
wasn't conducive to a long life.

Still, no sense in hanging around. I reloaded,
my shaking fingers barely able to manipulate the
speedloader. It was all I could do to tuck the
empty shells into a pocket, and I only remembered at the last moment to push the cylinder
closed instead of flicking it shut like a TV actor
would have.

I was about to take my leave—there was probably another waiting out for me, so I was going to
run down the other end of the alley, and make my

way back around the block—when I heard one still gasping.

"Healing draughts," he murmured, his fingers trying to walk his hand toward the body lying next to him. "There's healing draughts in Fendel's pouch. Feed them to me, swear to let me live, and I'll tell you something you want to know, even though it's too late."

"Talk first," I said, the pistol lined up with his head. One twitch would be his last. "How did you know it was me?"

"We've been . . . waiting for you. Ever since Toryn didn't report in. If he didn't report back, that meant he had come to terms with the lot of you, and was out chasing the Warrior, taking at least some of you away, leaving the rest vulnerable."

The rest? He couldn't mean Home—Home was well-protected—and that had to mean—

"Barony Cullinane," he said, and his smile was awful. "Team of assassins sent out, to leave a present for you to find when you get back. Find most of your women dead, one or two taken away, to be hurt every moment of every day until you come for them."

He started to tell me what they were going to do with them, in some detail. I stopped him.

I never really promised to let him live, and I wouldn't have kept the promise anyway. Which is probably what he was counting on, trading a world that was just pain for some surcease.

When I unwrapped my fingers from his throat, he was still smiling.

It took me less than a minute to make my way around the block quietly, and back to where Bren Adahan stood over the bodies of his three. His face was pale and sweaty, and he had one hand pressed against where a dark stain spread over his his left side, just above his hip, but he was in better shape than any of his playmates.

"What is it?" he said.

"I'll tell you on the way."

The top of the Anvil lay beneath a cloudy sky, starlight flickering through in only in a few broken places above.

"Is it possible we'll be in time?" Bren asked. A quick swig of healing draughts had taken the white out of his face, but my explanation had put it back.

I shrugged. "Anything's possible." What was certain is that we would be back earlier than we had intended. Maybe, just maybe, the assassins had been slowed by a few extra days. Maybe we would beat them to Castle Cullinane.

And maybe pigs would grow wings and become pigeons.

*Walter . . .* A distant voice sounded in my head.

*Ellegon? We've got troubles.*

It took me less time to tell it than I would have thought.

Wings beating the air, threatening to blow us from the surface, the dragon slammed down on the cold stone. *Get on board in ten seconds, or I'll leave without you.*

I scrambled up his leg, and onto his back, his scales cold beneath my fingers.

*Do you really think a few seconds is going to make a difference, Ellegon?*

*I expect to live a long time, Walter. I'll not live knowing that we wasted one second.*

Wind whipped dust into the air, and into my eyes.

# 14

## Ambush

The main thing about being a hero is to
know when to die.
—WILL ROGERS

Doing the best thing right away is
much better than doing the second-best
thing after much hesitation. I didn't say
it's easier, mind, just better.
—WALTER SLOVOTSKY

Bridge—the card game—was one of Lou Riccetti's innovations that hadn't caught on, and was largely a thing played by the Other Siders, with an exception or two.

Jason's tutor, Valeran, had been an exception. Jason didn't find the game interesting, although his father had insisted that he learn the rudiments of it. What he did find fascinating was the way that old Valeran played: the grizzled old warrior would sit erect at the table, never for a moment letting himself relax, never letting his concentration waver.

"The thing I like about it is that it reminds me of war without being bloody," he had once said. "Particularly when you have to take a view of the hand."

"Take a view of the hand?" Jason hadn't understood. "Peek at the other guy's cards?"

"No, no, no." Valeran had chuckled. "It's something you have to do when it looks like you're not going to make a contract. If you *need* for something to be true—say, for your left-hand enemy to be holding the Emperor, ten and three of Spades, precisely and only the King, Queen, and Lord of Sticks, and to be void in Jewels—then you assume that it's true, no matter how incredibly unlikely it is, because either the incredibly unlikely is about to happen or your hand is about to die horribly." He laughed, and Jason shook his head. "No, you don't understand, do you? Sometimes, see, the cards will lie the way they have to, and it all falls into place beautifully. Most of the time, though, you won't get what you need, and the hand dies." A rough hand felt at his cheek. "And then you can deal and play another hand. Which is how it's different from real life."

A low grunt to Jason's right became a scream, although whether it was in pain or fury was hard to say; he'd never heard Ahira cry out in either.

Jason didn't turn his head to look. It was all clear in his mind:

He would have to leave the bowmen to Ahira and Mikyn, and take the troop of six horsemen out himself.

Since that was manifestly impossible, he would need for Toryn to back him up, and since calling out an order—even if it were to be obeyed—would just alert the Pemburnians, everybody would have to do his part without being told.

Jason ducked behind his own horse, and came around toward the nearest of the horsemen. He batted aside the probing sword—this one was too tentative by half—and speared the horseman in the calf.

Not good enough. He shouted something, he was never quite sure what, as he slapped the horse across the flank with the flat of his blade, sending the horse galloping into startled flight.

From the corner of his eye, out at the edge of his vision, one of the bowmen was already falling off his horse, broken like a child's toy in Ahira's massive hands, but there wasn't time to take a look at the whole situation: another horseman was bearing down on him, lance targeting Jason's chest like it had eyes.

His father would have grabbed the lance and pulled it and the lancer from the saddle, but Jason wasn't his father, and didn't have that almost incredible strength.

But he did have a sword, and he could use its guard to catch the head of the lance, just behind the metal-clad point, and push it away.

Form was everything: as the horse came abreast, he took a single step to the right while his backstroke brought the tip of his sword up, into, and through the lancer's throat, letting him gallop past with blood fountaining between the clumsy fingers that suddenly came up to clutch at his own neck, the lance dropping.

Jason reached for the discarded lance, but another one blurred out of the edge of his vision and caught him on the side of his head. Nothing had ever hurt worse, but he couldn't, he didn't let the darkness around the rim of his mind creep in and haul him down: he brought up his sword, almost blindly, but managed to catch an attempted second blow just above the hilt.

He couldn't see. The blow had set bright sparks off in his head, and they were warring with the darkness, but he didn't need sight, not when he had a sword in his hand, in contact with the spear of an enemy: Jason slid his sword up the spear, in light contact, until the blade hit something, probably the lancer's heavy glove, and Jason turned the movement into a lunge, the point of his sword lodging somewhere in something.

He pulled it out with a twist, still blinded by the knock on the head, but decided that he'd

been in one place for too much time, so he more
staggered than ran to his right.

And collided *hard* with a tree; the rough bark
caught him on the face and in the middle of the
chest at the same time, his own momentum split-
ting his lip as it knocked the air right out of him,
sending his sword dropping from nerveless fingers as he fell backward.

He rolled around on the ground, trying to get
some breath in his lungs, some sight into his
eyes, or his sword into his hands, knowing that it
was all for nothing, that they had no chance at
all, but unwilling to give up as long as he could
move.

He had been clawing around on the ground for
several moments when he wondered why he
wasn't dead yet.

Jason raised his head, forcing himself to see
through the pain.

It was all over, or as all over as it was going
to be. There was a new path next to the road
where Ahira, berserk strength upon him, had
run through otherwise impenetrable brush. It
couldn't have even slowed him down much, or he
wouldn't have reached the spot next to where the
mounted bowmen waited. But he clearly had.
There weren't bowmen there anymore, just bodies, or parts of them, shallow pools of dark blood
already drawing flies. One arm had been flung

into the brush; it hung there, as though beckoning.

The dwarf squatted in front of the pile of pieces and offal, loud breath coming in noisy gasps.

A man lay in front of him, his neck at a sharp angle that told of it being broken, and it took Jason a moment to connect that with the tree limb in front of it. This had been Jason's first opponent, the horseman whose mount he had panicked into galloping flight.

Ahira looked up at Jason, and nodded, just once, and then his eyes swept by.

Toryn, unmarked, was standing over the inert body of another soldier, his sword probing, as though testing, then thrusting into and out of the torso, emerging dripping.

Marnea sat on Lord Pelester's chest, stained with blood from her face to her waist, the way she kept plunging a knife over and over again into the red mess that had been his face announcing that she hadn't been badly hurt, not physically, at least.

And Mikyn stood next to a tree, pinned neatly to it by an arrow that projected out of his dead, open mouth.

Sour vomit filled Jason's mouth, and splattered onto the dust and blood of the road.

* * *

"Enough for me."

Jason set one last rock into place and straightened, rubbing the relatively clean backs of his hands against his sweaty forehead. It would be nice to ride down to the Cirric and clean himself off, but once they got going, they had best get going quickly. The extra string of horses should make that easy.

The ground was hard and rocky, and the small shovel that had been part of Mikyn's gear was dull and ill-designed. Jason, his back aching from the tops of his shoulders to the base of his spine, finally decided on a shallow grave and a rocky cairn.

There would be time later to go through the rest of it, although it was hard to figure out who it ought to end up with. Mikyn's father was dead, and he had long ago abandoned Daherrin's raiding team, so there was no close buddy or family to give it to.

Marnea maybe.

He tried not to look at the heap of bodies barely concealed in the brush by the side of the road. That wasn't his problem. Getting away was his problem, but on horseback they should be able to outrun any likely pursuit, assuming there was going to be a further pursuit.

Using the flat of his battleaxe like a hammer, Ahira pounded a waist-high—chest-high for him—post into the ground at the head of Mikyn's cairn, while Marnea added another few stones.

Toryn's hands toyed with his horse's cinch-strap, as though he hadn't already tightened if half a dozen times. If Jason hadn't known better, he would have thought that the slaver was delay-ing taking his leave—but it was more likely that the motion was keeping his hands away from the hilt of his sword, and at this point he wanted to give neither Jason nor Ahira an excuse to violate their truce, what remained of it.

"It's been a pleasure, young Cullinane," he said. "Geas and all."

Ahira cocked his head to one side. "Does the geas still apply? I thought Mikyn's attack might have broken it."

"Did he attack me? Or did he just start to?" Toryn's fingers toyed with the ends of his mustache. "I couldn't say for sure, and I wouldn't want to bet my life what the spell would think." He smiled. "I know what Vair the Uncertain would say, something about how it would be un-wise to count on it either way, no?"

"Quite probably." Jason couldn't help smiling. He opened his mouth, closed it. The trouble was, he didn't want Toryn to leave, either. The—the slaver had been not only good in the fight, he had been reliable, he had made all the right moves in all the right directions, and without that, they would all have been dead. Jason was well-trained, and Ahira was a phenomenon, and yes, Marnea had taken out Pelester herself, but without Toryn, all three of them would have been spitted on a lance.

To hell with it. If he didn't say it, he would always regret it. "Ever consider a change of profession?"

He had half-expected Toryn to snicker, but not to sigh, shake his head, and then nod. "Yes, friend Jason, I have. I've been considering it for the past couple of days, ever since I realized that being involved with the two of you has been more fun than I've ever had in my life. It's much more fun than what I . . . do. I guess that's one of the reasons the Guildmaster picked me for this; he thought I'd fit in well enough with you that you wouldn't end up killing me."

"So?"

"So, I know things I haven't told you. Or, at least, think I do. It would be nice to be wrong for once, but in order for that—" he shook his head. "Never mind. If you knew what I know, you'd never forgive me for what I have done, and for what I have not said." Toryn put his foot in a stirrup and swung up to his horse's back. "And neither would I."

Jason watched him ride away for the longest time, wondering what kind of monster he had become that he found himself regretting Toryn's riding away more than Mikyn's death.

He turned to see Ahira nailing a small scrap of leather to Mikyn's headpost.

" 'The Warrior Lives,' eh?"

"Well, what would you leave as an inscription?" The dwarf smiled a little sadly. "Let's get going. We've a long ride back to your barony, and I don't want to take the most direct route. Not sure that Toryn won't have nobody waiting for us."

While Jason was trying to work his way through the compounded negatives to see if what Ahira said was what Jason knew the dwarf meant, Marnea spoke up.

"What's to become of me?" Marnea asked.

Jason wasn't sure if he heard a note of fear in her voice. "Well," he said with a smile, "if nothing else, we can always use another family retainer around the castle, one who's as handy with a knife as you are. Not that you're likely to see a lot of action there."

She grinned, wolfishly.

Ahira was already in the saddle of his gray gelding. "Let's get moving, people," he said.

*Sorry, Mikyn,* Jason thought. *But this could have ended with me a lot sorrier.*

# 15

## Heads on the Battlements

Nothing is so wretched or foolish as to anticipate misfortunes. What madness it is to be expecting evil before it comes.
—SENECA

The thing that feels best of all the things in the universe is either of my daughters' arms wrapped around my neck.
—WALTER SLOVOTSKY

Gray. Everything was gray, and damp, and had been forever.

I can remember, in the old days, one overcast day when Ellegon had made a pickup outside of Wehnest, and the dragon had climbed up through the clammy whiteness of a cloud layer to break through into golden sunshine, playing on white fluffiness below.

The top of the cloudscape hadn't been flat—it had been a white mountain range, where gentle cottony hillocks and valleys were broken by high-thrusting white mountains, some topped with impossible crests and spires that would have fallen had they been something more substantial than clouds.

But they had looked substantial, and if I blinked for a moment the cloudscape wasn't a bleached landscape, but was a roiling ocean frozen in time and space, lofty crests caught in midbreak above frosty troughs.

Out of concern for either his passenger's comfort or his own, that day Ellegon had gone to some trouble to avoid flying into clouds, and instead had followed the white terrain, flying fast, deep through snowy valleys, then climbing, climbing only to barely fit through a cottony pass in a snowy range up ahead.

It had been like making a run on the Death Star, I guess.

But not today. We had entered the clouds in the dark, and had flown through a black night that only became a ghastly, cold gray as daylight had dawned somewhere.

And the gray had gone on forever.

I could turn in the saddle just far enough to see Bren Adahan strapped in behind me, but the wind screamed by far too loudly for any conversation to be possible. In the old days, in a lighter mood, we could have talked via Ellegon—the dragon would relay comments, sometimes adding editorial remarks of his own.

But not now. I had tried a couple of times to say something to Ellegon, but there had been no response. It was as though I was just baggage, being carried through the wet and dark toward some horrid destination.

Please, God, let us be on time.

Looked at coldly, it all made horrible sense. The slavers had always overvalued Karl—and later me, and Ahira, and Jason—personally, preferring to think of their problems as simply a bunch of Other Side troublemakers rather than political changes that were going to transform the Eren regions, one way or another.

And since the times they had sent assassins after us had always failed, they had just waited, waited until a moment where they knew that we were away from those we loved, and that they were vulnerable in a small castle in a small barony in Holtun-Bieme. Just a matter of waiting until some sort of intelligence reported us all gone, and then they'd strike.

Brilliant. I had found out earlier than they had anticipated, but it was probably too late since the word had gotten out at all. The assassins had been dispatched the moment they first knew all of us were away, and—

—and I couldn't think of what would happen next. They would have set things up so that my only chance to free whoever was left alive would be to walk into a trap that I had no chance of walking out of.

So be it, I decided. I'd have to work it so that they'd let go of whoever they were holding, but the slavers couldn't make everybody walk into a death trap. There were people I could count on, like Durine, Kethol, and Pirojil, and maybe Daherrin.

They would avenge all of us.

That thought didn't dispel the grayness. All I could think of was what an idiot I'd been, leaving most of what I loved alone and vulnerable, trusting to a few soldiers and my reputation to protect them.

Idiot. I was an—

The dragon broke through the clouds above Castle Cullinane, and even from this height I could see the heads mounted on pikes on the battlement below.

I had never heard a dragon scream before; flame flared loud, roaring hot, from Ellegon's massive jaws, the speed of his flight washing too much heat back over me, so much so that I had to huddle deep in my cloak to avoid getting burned.

But the fire stopped, and I heard a distant laughter in my mind that I couldn't possibly have been close enough to hear with my ears, and Ellegon swooped out of the sky like a hawk, his fast-moving wings pounding the air as he braked just in time to prevent us from smashing ourselves against the stones of the courtyard.

*The heads on the battlements,* Ellegon said in my mind, in sweet words I'll never forget, *all have *beards*.*

There had been some damage, but just around the edges. The remnants of a ladder lay next to the eastern wall; it was mainly just a pile of sticks, as though some careless, angry giant had ripped it off and crushed it. There were scorch marks on the wall above the main kitchen's windows, and a distant rotting smell that I didn't like to think about.

But a familiar little face peeked out of the darkness of an entrance: Andy, one arm in a sling, was just inside the doorway, a vague smile on her face, insolently leaning against the wall.

I heard "Hi, Daddy," and my baby daughter was already slapping her hands against the dragon's scaly side before my trembling fingers could release me from my harness and lower me to the ground. "Everybody's okay."

Things got a little fuzzy after that. I do remember not being bothered by the way that Bren Adahan swooped up Kirah into his arms, and the sounds of his sobbing mixed with his laughter, and I remember hurting both of us when I hugged

Janie—the pistol stuck into her belt pressed too hard against both of our hips.

And maybe most of all I remember Aeia, her breath warm in my ear. "I *told* you I'd wait for you." And I will never forget how good it felt to have her mouth warm on mine.

But it wasn't all solemn; I laugh when I remember Doria's words of greeting: "I don't know what you're crying about, Walter. We're the ones who had to clean this all up."


You want details? I wanted details.

Which is all I got, and only bit by bit.


Like:

Andy, midevening, her face lit almost demonically by the only light in the room, a flickering oil lamp on the table at her elbow. She sat back in an overstuffed easy chair, still wearing her leathers, one leather-encased leg thrown carelessly over the chair's arm. It was a nice leg. "I was just outside my room, to take my boots off and go to bed, when one of the bastards snaked his arm around my neck. What he got started with a bootheel raked down his shin from knee to ankle, and ended sometime later with his head on a pole." She shrugged. "If he'd wanted me dead, he could have had that. Tried to get fancy; figured he'd play for a while first." She smiled. "Bad choice."

* * *

Like:

Janie, late at night in the watchtower on the southwest corner of the castle's wall, her eyes on the night, a bowl of iced sweetlemon glacé precariously balanced on the rail. I wasn't prepared to believe that the killings hadn't affected her, but she wasn't ready to discuss it. Just:

"Well, Jason left his spare pistol with me, and I don't think they were ready to deal with a six-shooter." She shrugged. "And then there were these two." She bent to pat the head of Nick, who gazed lovingly up at her, while Nora eyed me with something between distrust and distaste.

I reached out to put an arm around Janie's waist, but Nora's ears flattened until Janie shook her head and gestured at Nora to be still.

"Nice doggies," I said.

"Depends on if you play nice or not." Janie smiled.


Like:

Fat U'len in her kitchen just before dawn, her cleaver beating a rapid tattoo against her cutting board, shredding a piece of ham into strips that looked like short, pink noodles. "Kirah and my Doranne were here in the kitchen when two of them broke in, and one of them went for the baby." She gestured over to the tiny mattress and blanket in the corner, separated from the stove by a wooden latticework that let the heat keep the sleeper warm. "I didn't do much," she said, as her massive arms worked the pump over the sink, more sluicing off than rinsing an onion. A quick stroke took off its roots, another its head, and a quick slice-and-flick removed the brown outer skin. Another series of rapid strokes against the cutting board made the onion appear to fly apart, leaving behind only a neat little minced pile. "Kirah had her knitting with her, and she pulled out a pair of knitting needles and jumped one of them, which gave me enough time to get to my cleaver," she said, gently breaking an egg against the blade, economically dropping the yolk and white into a bowl and in the same motion tossing the shells into the garbage bin. "Just as happy we had the healing draughts handy," she said. "She got herself hurt, although he got himself hurt more. Now, if I'm going to make you an omelette, you'd better eat it all, understood?" She gestured with the cleaver. "Understood?"

"Yes'm."

Like: Doria, once again curled up on her chair in the foyer. "You can give Aeia a lot of the credit. Her and Andy. She heard somebody out in the hall trying to walk too quietly, and got me out of my room. It was about that time that Andy showed up, armed for bear, ready for blood. She and Aeia were going to get Kirah and the baby up from downstairs when it all hit the fan." She patted at my leg. "We would have liked having you around, Walter, but we didn't need you." She shrugged, and smiled, and hugged me. "Sorry if that makes you feel unwanted."

Like: Doranne at the breakfast table, more stabbing at than eating her raisin-spotted porridge. "Bad man said he was going to hurt me. Mommy and U'len stopped him, and Mommy told me not to look." She looked up at me and smiled. "It's okay, Daddy. Medicine made Mommy better, and they wouldn't give medicine to the bad man."

Like: Aeia in our bed, laughing and sweaty above me, the tips of her hair like silk against my face. "Walter, you worry too much."

Out in the night, flame roared skyward, partly in laughter, partly in relief.

# 16

# The Dream Is the Same

Tyranny and anarchy are never far
asunder.

—JEREMY BENTHAM

Give me a place to stand, and I'll
probably move along anyway.

—WALTER SLOVOTSKY

The nightmare is always the same:

*We're trying to make our escape from Hell, millions of us running through the immense castle's unbelievably long corridors, past the empty rooms, toward the main gate, and safety.*

*Too many of us, no matter how much the corridor widens, there's always too many of us; I'm constantly being scraped against the red-hot walls, blisters flaring and bursting with a horrid pain that doesn't go away even as they disappear.*

*Everybody I've ever loved is there, and some of them look to me for guidance, as though I'm supposed to know something. What the hell do they want of me?*

*Behind us, the demons follow: silent men in black, blades flowering from their fingertips, seeking innocent flesh.*

*We follow the crowd as it plunges into a stairwell at the end of the corridor and down through the endless spiral of staircase that I hope leads to safety, as though safety is a place.*

*They're all swept away from me: Janie, reaching out a hand to bring her baby sister along; Aeia, mouthing a promise to wait for me; Doria, smiling reassuringly as she vanishes in the crowd; Kirah, with a quick squeeze on my arm that speaks of a lingering sort of affection.*

*"Once more," Karl says, a hand clasped to my shoulder. "One last time, Walter."*

*And then what, asshole?*

*They all line up, blocking the corridor. All the old ones, too old to do this, but unwilling to give in to age, any more than they'd accept defeat by any other enemy.*

*"But we're not here," old Jonas Salk says, his right hand shattering a demon with just a gesture, "this is just your dream, just a figment of your imagination. I'd be in my lab, where I belong."*

*Eleanor Roosevelt rends another demon with her fingers, and tosses it aside. "And I would be giving speeches, I trust, where they would be listened to. That's my place, Walter."*

*Sister Berthe reaches out a gentle hand to pat my shoulder, then pulls the ruler out of her habit and slaps another demon into dust. "I taught you what a metaphor is, Walter. That's all your dreams are. You don't have to be so," she sniffs, "literal all the time."*

*The old sailor is there, his beard white as fleece against his lined, leathery face, the scar on his leg, taking his position next to me—*

*Omygod. I know who he is, finally.*

*" 'Though much is taken, much remains,' " I say to him, and he smiles.*

*"Some work of noble note," he says, "but it need not be your work of yesterday." He looks down at me, concerned. "You're getting a bit too old for this, Cricket," he says, his face my father's, his voice Big Mike's. "You can't be a young stud all your life. Time to learn how to be an older stud, eh?"*

And then I wake up.

Doria and Bren Adahan were downstairs in a room off the main corridor that had always been called the Prince's Den for no reason that anybody I knew of knew.

She was wearing a black robe, as though she had come from bed, but there was a suspicious bulge at the waistline under it that made me decide this was no accident.

Bren looked like an ad for some sort of post-coital clothing catalogue: a thin, loose, long cotton shirt open to the waist, the high collar almost covering a bite mark at the base of his neck.

He smiled a greeting, and I returned it as I plopped down in the chair next to Doria's.

"Late-night crowd, eh?" I asked as I reached for a bit of sweetroll on the plate by her elbow.

Doria shrugged her shoulders. They were nice shoulders. "And you've been dreaming again. Care to talk about it?"

"Ulysses," I said. "I've been dreaming of all the old ones, starting with Ulysses."

At the edge of my vision, Bren's forehead wrinkled, but Doria nodded. " 'To sail beyond the sunset,' eh?" She turned to Bren. "It's a poem some of us studied, about an old king, too old for wandering and adventuring, who sets out again, because even if he's not what he once was . . ." She closed her eyes for a moment.

" 'Tho' much is taken,' " she said, opening her eyes and looking at me, " 'much abides; and tho'

" 'We are not now that strength which in old days

" 'Moved earth and heaven; that which we are, we are . . .' " Her voice trailed off.

It had been too many years since Sister Berthe

had taught me the poem, but the years didn't matter.

" '. . . that which we are, we are;

" 'One equal temper of heroic hearts,

" 'Made weak by time and fate, but strong in will

" 'To strive, to seek, to find, and not to yield.' "
I shrugged. "Sorry; I can't give it all up. And I'm not going to try."

She nodded. "So, you're leaving us?" Doria was always a step or two beyond me.

"Yes, and no." I thought about it for a moment, and thought about how neither Bren nor I was meeting the other's eyes, and how that wasn't because we were angry or anything, but because we'd divided the world into halves, his to watch out for and mine.

I didn't particularly like him, and I very much didn't like the thought of Kirah lying warm in his arms at night, but sometimes it doesn't matter even to me what I like.

"The point isn't to keep doing what you've been doing until you get too old for it, but to keep making yourself useful. I'm starting to slow down, and while I'm more than a match for most, I'm not a match for all. 'Tho' much is taken, much abides'—I'm going to have to leave this jumping out of windows and fighting in alleyways for the younger folks sooner or later, and I'd better get used to the idea that that's a good thing, not a bad thing. There's other things I can do, and not necessarily boring ones, either."

Doria smiled. "Still a little fight in the old boy, eh?"

"Maybe." I shrugged.

*You up for a night flight tomorrow night?* I asked Ellegon.

*Depends where, I suppose. Oh, sure. Why not? What have you got in mind?*

*Job interview.*

Bren looked over at me, and tilted his head to one side. "You want some company?"

I nodded. "I was sort of counting on it."

# 17

## Job Interview

It is not enough to be busy; so are the
ants. The question is: What are we busy
about?
—HENRY DAVID THOREAU

While it doesn't get the good press that
hard work and industry get, laziness is a
talent to be cultivated, like any other.
—WALTER SLOVOTSKY

The room was dark, almost completely dark, lit
only by shreds of distant lantern light leaking in
under the door to the hallway outside. Enough
for me, mind; my night vision has always been
good, and I'd taken the precaution of blindfolding
myself on the trip over to give my eyes plenty of
time to adapt to the dark. Ellegon had dropped us
off on the roof of the donjon quite silently before
more noisily arriving in the courtyard, and it had

hardly been any trouble at all to work our way down from the top and into the room.

He lay alone in his massive bed, which made things simpler. I mean, we could have handled it if he had company, but I liked it this way.

Bren Adahan grinned wolfishly as he drew his sword and lightly, gently touched the sleeping Emperor on the chest.

Give him credit: Thomen came awake instantly, and neither cried out nor reached for the hidden flintlock pistol that had been tucked under his mattress, but now was displayed quite prominently in my belt.

"Good evening, Your Majesty," Bren said, striking a match and lighting Thomen's bedside lantern. Golden light flared, casting shadows all about the room, lighting Bren's face demonically from below.

Thomen's head jerked around, first toward him, and then toward me. His beard was all crushed and his mustache kind of askew, as though he'd been sleeping, which seemed reasonable, since he'd been sleeping. I would have offered him a comb, a brush, and a few minutes to get himself together, but that would have ruined the effect.

"We've come about a couple of jobs," I said. "I think you need a pair of special representatives, for difficult political problems. Care to review my qualifications?"

Sometime or another, Thomen had learned to be a politician; I couldn't tell anything by the expression on his face. "I had thought I'd offered you such a position, not too long ago."

I shook my head. "No. I'm not talking about running around playing catch every time your mother finds something that likes to throw spears. We may have other projects in the fire, every now and then."

"Seems likely. When things quiet down in Pandathaway, I intend to kill whoever it is that sent assassins after Kirah and her daughters," Bren said, without heat, in the quiet way that a death sentence is passed.

"Make that 'we intend'—but save the details for later," I said to shut him up, then turned back to Thomen. "We'll work for you, not your mother; and that means we report to you, and not to your mother."

"Whenever we want to," Bren put in. "Even in the middle of the night."

Thomen's smile was crooked. "You seem to have arranged that part of it already."

I rubbed at the small of my back. "I'm starting to get too old to be jumping in and out of windows. Next time I get to walk in, through the door. Any time, night or day. That's for a starter."

"And?"

"And, him." I jerked my thumb at Bren. "He sits in for you when you're taking some time off."

"The Biemish barons will love that," Thomen said, sarcastically.

I smiled. "I've been thinking about that, and I've got a few ideas about how to make them like it better."

"You do?"

"I do."

In fact, with the idea properly sold, the Biemish barons would like it better if it were a Holt occupying the office, as there was no possibility of a Holt seizing permanent power. The Furnael dynasty wasn't even a generation old, and the Biemish barons were certainly nervous about other Biemish barons taking the throne. But I'd save that for later.

"In any case," I went on, "you do take some time off—all work and no play makes Thomen a dull Emperor. You need to spend more time with your butt in a saddle and less with it on a throne. Bren will keep the throne warm for you."

"And you?"

"I'll run important errands for you, with Bren when he's available, but with whatever support I think necessary: a few bodyguards, a troop from the House Guard, or a baronial army. And a nice title—Imperial Proctor, maybe. Something that suggests it'd be real unhandy if anything were to happen to me."

"I take it there's more."

"Sure. Our families live in the castle, here,

under your protection, when we aren't based out of Little Pittsburgh and Castle Adahan. They come and they go as they please, with Imperial troops for thcir security, too." I turned to Bren. "What next?"

"Next, we need to arrange a divorce," Bren said. "And a marriage, as well. Or is it two marriages?" He looked over at me.

"I haven't exactly asked her, yet," I said. "I sort of figured I'd have to dispose of one wife before I take on another one, eh?"

Bren laughed.

And, after a moment, so did Thomen. "Imperial Proctor, eh? Well, true enough, I could find some work for you."

"Some work of noble note, eh?"

He looked at me kind of funny. "Rather." And then he smiled. "One thing, though?"

"Yes?"

"I don't care where it is, or what happened to it, but I want my candelabra back. Soon."

"Done."


The guards in the entranceway probably would have done something if the Emperor himself, in dressing gown and sandals, hadn't let us out of the Imperial sleeping chambers, but under the circumstances, about the only thing they could do was glare.

And salute, once matters were properly explained to them. Imperial Proctor, eh?

As we walked down the hall toward the long, winding staircase, Bren Adahan chuckled. "I don't know as I believe in this new, er, conservative policy of yours. Seems to me we might have wanted to have a backup plan, if the Emperor hadn't been so cooperative, or if he hadn't meant what he said."

Well, I could have told him about how I'd asked Ellegon to monitor Thomen for honesty, and how the dragon was ready to pick us up on the roof where he'd dropped us off, but I don't like to give away all my secrets.

*It would ruin the effect, at that.*

*Shh.* "I always have a backup plan handy, Bren."

He snorted. "Dying horribly, at length, and in great pain, is not a plan."

I shrugged. "Well, it's not a good one." I yawned. "Any idea where I can go to get some sleep?"

# L'ENVOI I

## Home Again

Eternal rest sounds comforting in the
pulpit; well, you try it once, and see how
heavy time will hang on your hands.
—MARK TWAIN

The hot bath is an art form, and one I
wish I had the time to practice more
assiduously.
—WALTER SLOVOTSKY

Even after five days back home, the best thing in
the world was to sit back in the hot bath and let
the almost scalding water soak the dirt out of his
pores and the ache out of his bones.

"Ahira?" Jason Cullinane called out. "It's starting to cool again."

In a moment, the dwarf appeared, a long set of
tongs holding a red-hot piece of scrap iron, which
he plunged into the water. The steam momentar-

ily hid his face and Jason quickly kicked water at the iron to move the heat around.

Much better. "Thanks."

Things were settling down, for the time being. Walter and Bren were moving their families over to Biemestren within the next tenday, which was going to make things a bit quiet around here. Janie was going to stay on for a while, which was nice, although Marnea's presence probably had a lot to do with that.

There had been rumors of some strange creatures to the south and west again. Probably some remnant of what had strayed out of Faerie; probably a good idea to go look into it.

He said as much to the dwarf.

Ahira nodded. "In a few weeks. I want some time with the kids before we go. Your mother's going to want to come along, you know."

Jason shrugged. There were worse things in the world than that, although he really would have wanted a bit larger group.

Still . . .

Ahira flashed a broad smile, then turned to leave. "If you'll excuse me, I've got a knife I'm working on."

"Enjoy."

Doria poked her head in through the door. "Somebody here to see you."

"Imperial messenger?"

She shook her head. "Won't give a name. Tall,

a bit on the skinny side, maybe. Neat beard. Kind of cute, if you like that type." She smiled. "I like that type. Says you'll want to see him."

Toryn—"You left him alone?"

"The hilt of his sword looked a little too well worn for that, and if it hadn't, it would have looked too new, or too perfect." She smiled. "So he's under guard, disarmed, in manacles, if you call that alone. I was wondering if you wanted to wait to see him until you got out—"

Jason was already out of the bath, wrapping a towel about his waist and seizing up his weapons belt before following Ahira out into the day.

Toryn was standing out near the main entrance, trying his best to look insouciant despite the iron manacles and the stern-eyed guards.

"New style of dress?" he asked.

"What are you doing here?"

Toryn pursed his lips for a moment, as though considering, then shrugged. "Truth to tell, I didn't want to discuss in front of the Guildmaster how I didn't even try to kill the both of you, when you were so winded and vulnerable after the fight with Pelester, and the geas possibly broken. He wasn't likely to believe that it was impossible for me, and might have insisted on running me over to Wizard's Guildhall for a truth spell." Toryn shrugged. "And that might have been awkward. I decided to hope," he said, "that the assassins might have failed, so I decided to head this way, rather than back to Pandathaway."

"And if they hadn't failed, you would have—"

"—turned my horse around and ridden away," Toryn said, "and rather quickly, at that. But the word in all the villages is that they did fail, and I thought that under the circumstances, you might find my . . . omissions forgivable," he said, "or at the very least give me a running start." He brought his manacled hands up, as though studying his manicure. "Alternately, we could find the nearest Spider and have him attest to my truthfulness, and then we might see if there's something . . . interesting to do."

Jason cocked his head to one side. "What makes you think we've got something on?"

Toryn smiled. "Just a hunch."

# L'ENVOI II

## Home Again

Home is where the heart is.
                    —PLINY THE ELDER

No, wherever *she* is, wherever my kids
are, that's home. And if that sounds a
bit too sentimental, well, I'll just have to
live with it.
                    —WALTER SLOVOTSKY

The dreams are always different, these days. But
the days have been getting kind of hectic.

Aeia says, well—I'll tell you about it sometime.
Trust me.

# By Way of an Appendix

Since this is the poem that's running—sometimes amok—through Walter's subconscious throughout the novel, and since I couldn't quite talk Doria and Walter into reciting all of it in Chapter 16—I tried, honest, but they've got minds of their own—I thought I'd save you the trouble of looking it up.

It's one of my favorites.

—J.R.

**Ulysses**
*by Alfred, Lord Tennyson*

It little profits that an idle king,
By this still hearth, among these barren
   crags,
Match'd with an agéd wife, I mete and dole
Unequal laws unto a savage race,
That hoard, and sleep, and feed, and know
   not me.
I cannot rest from travel: I will drink
Life to the lees: all times I have enjoy'd
Greatly, have suffer'd greatly, both with
   those
That loved me, and alone; on shore, and
   when
Thro' scudding drifts the rainy Hyades
Vext the dim sea: I am become a name;
For always roaming with a hungry heart
Much have I seen and known; cities of men
And manners, climates, councils,
   governments,
Myself not least, but honour'd of them all;
And drunk delight of battle with my peers,
Far on the ringing plains of windy Troy.
I am a part of all that I have met;
Yet all experience is an arch wherethro'
Gleams that untravell'd world, whose margin
   fades
For ever and for ever when I move.

How dull it is to pause, to make an end,
To rust unburnish'd, not to shine in use!
As tho' to breathe were life. Life piled on life
Were all too little, and of one to me
Little remains: but every hour is saved
From that eternal silence, something more,
A bringer of new things; and vile it were
For some three suns to store and hoard
  myself,
And this grey spirit yearning in desire
To follow knowledge, like a sinking star,
Beyond the utmost bound of human
  thought.

This is my son, mine own Telemachus,
To whom I leave the sceptre and the isle—
Well-loved of me, discerning to fulfil
This labour, by slow prudence to make mild
A rugged people, and thro' soft degrees
Subdue them to the useful and the good.
Most blameless is he, centred in the sphere
Of common duties, decent not to fail
In offices of tenderness, and pay
Meet adoration to my household gods,
When I am gone. He works his work, I
  mine.

There lies the port: the vessel puffs her sail:
There gloom the dark broad seas. My
  mariners,

Souls that have toil'd, and wrought, and
   thought with me—
That ever with a frolic welcome took
The thunder and the sunshine, and opposed
Free hearts, free foreheads—you and I are
   old;
Old age hath yet his honour and his toil;
Death closes all: but something ere the end,
Some work of noble note, may yet be done,
Not unbecoming men that strove with
   Gods.
The lights begin to twinkle from the rocks:
The long day wanes: the slow moon climbs:
   the deep
Moans round with many voices. Come, my
   friends,
'Tis not too late to seek a newer world.
Push off, and sitting well in order smite
The sounding furrows; for my purpose holds
To sail beyond the sunset, and the baths
Of all the western stars, until I die.
It may be that the gulfs will wash us down:
It may be we shall touch the Happy Isles,
And see the great Achilles, whom we knew.
Tho' much is taken, much abides; and tho'
We are not now that strength which in old
   days
Moved earth and heaven; that which we are,
   we are;

One equal temper of heroic hearts,
Made weak by time and fate, but strong in
   will
To strive, to seek, to find, and not to yield.

# Author's Afterword

As always, Walter's heroes are his own. Where real people, such as Jonas Salk, or Golda Meir, or Robert Heinlein, appear in his dream sequences, the intention is to give a fictional impression of Walter's view of them, not necessarily of mine— which in those cases, among others, is even more respectful.

Return to the origins of the Guardians of the Flame

# THE SLEEPING DRAGON

*Captives of Sorcery* . . .

It began as just another evening of fantasy gaming, with James, Karl, Andrea, and the rest ready to assume their various roles as wizard, cleric, warrior, or thief. But sorcerous gamemaster Professor Deighton had something else planned for this unsuspecting group of college students. And the "game" soon became a matter of life and death as the seven adventurers found themselves transported to an alternate world and into the bodies of the actual characters they had been pretending to be.

Cast into a land where magic worked all too well, dragons were a fire-breathing menace, and only those quick enough with a sword or their wits survived, the young gamers faced a terrible task. For the only way they would ever see Earth again was if they could find the legendary Gate Between Worlds—a place guarded by the most terrifying and deadly enemy of all. . . .

# THE SWORD AND THE CHAIN

*Warrior, Wizard, Dwarf, Thief, and Master Builder—*

all of them had chosen this world as their destiny, a realm where dragons were only too real and magic, not science, was the law of the land. Karl, Andrea, Ahira, Walter, and Lou knew there was no going back to twentieth-century America now. Instead, they were stranded in a time and place where only healing spells and their own wits stood between them and the sharp, deadly edge of a slaver's blade.

But even if they could have returned home by some sorcerous trick, all of them would have refused the chance, bound by their pledge to bring this incredible realm the one treasure it lacked—freedom! But leagued against them in their fight were the entire forces of both the Wizards and the Slavers guilds. And, in this world where a wrong step or a twisted spell could transform friend into foe, how could Karl and his band survive long enough to fulfill their pledge?

# THE SILVER CROWN

*Magic's Deadly Edge*

The stronghold called Home was prospering, and Karl's dream of bringing freedom to everyone in this land peopled by wizards and warriors, lords and slaves, dwarfs and elves and dragons was at last coming true. But by attacking slaver caravans, by offering Home as a haven to any eager to throw off their chains, Karl, Andrea, Ahira, and their comrades had made many powerful enemies.

Led by the evil Ahrmin, the Slaver's Guild was stirring the kingdoms into a bloody war in which Karl and his friends might soon have to choose sides. And the elfin kingdom of Therranj claimed Karl's valley sanctuary as part of its own territory and was demanding both tribute and loyalty from the people of Home.

Caught between slaver forces armed with a magical new weapon and elves attempting to steal the treasured secret of gunpowder, could Karl's human, dwarf, elf, and dragon warriors keep the walls of Home standing for long?

# THE HEIR APPARENT

*Slaver's Gambit!*

Karl Cullinane and his fellow Earth-exiles Andrea, Ahira, Walter, and Lou had succeeded beyond their wildest expectations in the years since a wizard's spell had cast them into an alternate world where magic and dragons were real. Now Karl was Emperor and his son Jason was of an age to begin learning the realities of war and leadership. And with the aid of dwarves, elves, humans, and one sarcastic dragon, Karl and his friends had freed many from the evil specter of slavery and were pledged to fight till slavery was at an end. But their actions had made them some extremely powerful enemies, chief among whom was Ahrmin of the Slaver's Guild.

And for Ahrmin the time for final reckoning had at least arrived. With or without the aid of the Guild, he would draw sword and take blood vengeance on Karl and Jason Cullinane and all they held dear. . . .

# THE WARRIOR LIVES

*Karl Cullinane Is Dead . . . Or Is He?*

When Karl Cullinane, warrior, champion of the forces fighting the Slaver's Guild, and Emperor, is declared dead, Jason, his son and heir, must take on the responsibilities of leadership. Now trying to fill his father's legendary shoes, he commands the inner circle of warriors and the dragon Ellegon to track down the deadly Slaver's Guild. But soon rumors surface about unauthorized raids. The appearance of a dwarf brings untimely death to those who traffic in human suffering. And a cryptic message is left on the corpses of the enemy—"The Warrior Lives!" Could it be—against all odds—that Karl and his comrades have survived? Jason must learn the truth . . . and to do so he will use the very same tactics his father would have used. . . .

# THE ROAD TO EHVENOR

*A Quest into the Heart of Magic*

Something is not all right with This Side, the
alternate world where the guardians find
themselves. Magic—or at least a rumor of it—is
creeping out of Faerie at the border town of
Ehvenor. And even though Jason Cullinane, son
of the legendary Karl, has not yet settled into his
new role as baron, he and his companions cannot
ignore the pleas of those they were sworn to
protect. So when great sea serpents rise from the
ocean depths, when livestock is swallowed whole
by an unseen menace, and when wolfpacks
suddenly have more in common with
shapechangers then canines, Jason has no choice
but to ride to the rescue with his inner circle of
warriors—and challenge the forces of chaos
before they gain a foothold in the human lands.

ROC

# THE BEST IN SCIENCE FICTION
# AND FANTASY

If you and/or a friend would like to receive the *ROC Advance*, a bimonthly newsletter featuring all the newest and hottest ROC books and authors, on a complimentary basis, please fill out this form and return it to:

**ROC Books/Penguin USA**
375 Hudson Street
New York, NY 10014

Your Address
Name _____
Street _____ Apt. # _____
City _____ State _____ Zip _____

Friend's Address
Name _____
Street _____ Apt. # _____
City _____ State _____ Zip _____